WHEN THE BASIL BOLTS

By JJ Dayton

I0619750

Dedico este libro a mi Viejo y a mi familia aunque dudo que lo leyan. A lo mejor, no deben de leerlo porque es romance y un poco "racy," es decir, picante.

Cerritos Books

TABLE of CONTENTS

Chapter 1: A New Job

Ellie sat on her back steps, contemplating the herb garden that she'd been so carefully tending for the past month since moving back to Texas. She didn't know when she'd get used to having to plant things so early and again in the fall. Her gardener's mind was still working with the northern rhythms of nature that had a short, but productive summer season. Here, with the sweltering Texas summer facing her, she'd listened to local comments about getting her garden in early and had planted seeds and plants in April.

Looking at her cilantro and basil, she saw it was time to take some cuttings to hang to dry to use months later in winter when her herb garden was finally finished for the season. She wanted to cut leaves soon, especially the basil; it gets so bitter after it bolts and hers looked like it was ready to. Locals had told her that some of her herbs would make it through the long, hot summer till fall and would thrive again. Ellie wondered if that could be true. It was already hot and getting humid and she thought she could see tiny flower buds forming on her herbs. Her dog Duke came up and, seeing that she seemed busy, gave her knee a nudge and then circled once and sat down by her feet, curled up to rest his nose on his paws that he placed right beside her foot and on one of her other feet.

Knowing it was time to get her head wrapped around deciding about working this summer, Ellie ran through the pros and cons yet one more time. Among the pros, the money she'd earn stood out at the top of the list. Among the con's, having to commit herself to anything with a daily routine also stood out at the top of the negatives. She'd gotten used to doing nothing for the past year when she'd recovered from her bout with cancer, sold her house and moved back to Texas. Many, many changes in a relatively short period of time had left her feeling rudderless.

'Why can't I make up my mind?! I'm tired of not doing anything, but it's so seductive, that feeling of just floating along. But I'm tired of having no purpose. I don't even do any volunteer work at all. I don't know who I am anymore, I guess. Crap. I'm tired of being tired. I'm tired of being bored. I don't know why it's so damn hard to just make up my mind and do something for a change,' Ellie groaned and rubbed her forehead, feeling a tension headache coming on.

"That's it. I'm going to go online and see if there are any classes I can teach this summer. Forget that it's been ten years since I've been in the classroom. I can do this!" Ellie said to Duke as she got up, her herbs forgotten.

Following up on her decision, Ellie dutifully researched on her computer to see what she could find at such short notice that it didn't involve too much driving. Glad that she did find two promising openings, she then worked on finding all the necessary paperwork and scanning certificates and transcripts into her computer and then filling out the online applications and submitting

7

them for two positions. She also saw an administrator's position but decided to wait on that one as her last option if nothing panned out from her two teaching applications. She had the credentials to be an administrator but felt like at this juncture in her life that she needed to roll up her sleeves and jump back into teaching without the added responsibilities of being the boss running the show.

Duke looked up at Ellie from his spot beside the couch, noticing a change in his mistress and wondering what was going on, if he should get excited because they were going for a car ride or a walk. When he noticed that Ellie seemed to be just thinking and not getting up to go anywhere, he figured he'd just stay put and watch her for a while. This was the most enthusiasm she'd shown in a while though and he was glad to think she was more like her old self.

Ellie checked her computer after lunch and was excited to see that she'd had one reply to her application. When she opened it, the director of the adult education program at the local junior college had emailed her that he wanted her to come in for an interview as soon as possible, giving her his phone number to call to schedule.

'That's good news, right? If so, why is my stomach in knots? I just got emailed to set up an interview and that's a good thing if I want this job. Yes? Oh, crap. Maybe I was too hasty. I should have just thought about it a little longer. But I knew that if there were any openings this late before summer school typically begins, they would be definite and the schools eager to hire. I did this once right before school and got job offers right away. It was the desperation time for principals wanting to have teachers in classrooms rather than subs. Hopefully, it will work again and I'll get hired.'

Ellie called Mr. Morris to schedule her interview and was surprised when he asked her if she could come over that same afternoon around three. Agreeing to see him in a few hours, Ellie started to feel nervous when she realized she hadn't been on a serious full-time job interview in a dozen years. She had worked part time for a small private college in upstate New York a few years ago, but she'd left there more than three years past and didn't feel like her interviewing skills were honed and ready. *'Honed?! That's hilarious and slightly idiotic to even think that. Ha!'*

Ellie arrived ten minutes early, planning to spend the time reviewing her resume to reacquaint herself with the particulars and realized she had really jumped rashly into this idea of getting a job. She felt as nervous as she had many years ago for her first job interview for a "real" job, which she didn't get after only a barely fair performance on her part. She didn't want to feel like a fool and had decided that she did want to give this a try. She had nothing to lose and might just enjoy herself. Teaching had always been fun years ago.

Mr. Morris heard that Ellie was outside and appeared in the waiting area to show her in himself. *'So much for using this time to prep. Oh well.'*

"I appreciate your coming in this afternoon to interview, Ellie. May I call you Ellie, Mrs. Thompson?"

"Yes, of course, Mr. Morris," Ellie said while wondering to herself, *'and am I going to call you by your first name, young man? Crap, I must be at least fifteen years older than he is.'*

Maybe the incongruity of the situation finally struck him because Mr. Morris looked uncomfortable and quickly said, "You must call me Dave, Ellie."

"Well, Dave. It's nice to meet you," Ellie said in the conversational void, feeling like she was stepping back into her administrator role to help him through the interview since it felt like he was floundering.

"Er, yes. I do have to say I was quite impressed by your credentials and experience, Ellie. We don't often get someone with your job history applying for Adult Basic Education positions here. I hate to say it, but you are definitely overqualified for any job opening I have," Dave said reluctantly and looked at Ellie to see what her reply would be.

"Dave, as you can see, I've been taking a break for the last few years and have recently moved back to Texas and decided I wanted to get back into working and I always enjoyed adult education. It was my favorite teaching position earlier in my career. When I saw the job listing, I thought it would be perfect."

"Hmm. I see. I also see here that you have your Masters in English as a Second Language and did the coursework and received your public-school administration certificate. Additionally, you are certified in high school Spanish and English as well as elementary through seventh grade. How does that relate to this position?"

"Well, Dave. I've taught ESL to students aged 5-65 along with GED math and basic literacy. I've also taught high school

English, grades 9-12 and Spanish I, II and III. I've written curriculum guides and developed courses that got TEA approval for my district. My elementary certification equipped me with the skills to teach early literacy and reading which directly relates to Adult Basic Education. I think all of those are relevant because I do have training in teaching reading, writing, math and ESL, all of which are represented in your adult ed program. Is that correct?"

"Yes, Ellie. I think your experience makes you uniquely qualified for a job in our program. I would like to propose something a little different than what I posted though. I'd like to hire you as interim director with teaching duties also. I think you have the knowhow to lead the program as well as teach a few classes if you're interested in something like I've described."

Surprised, Ellie just looked at Dave for a moment and then said, "Wow. That wasn't what I expected, Dave."

"I realize this might be a shock, but I need an administrator who's also qualified to teach and can comfortably wear both hats. I think you'd be perfect for that position. Also, the salary is double what the teaching position pays."

"Well, Dave. That does put it in a different light. Maybe you could explain more about the position and the program so I could learn enough to decide on your offer," Ellie said after a moment's hesitation.

After Dave went into the specifics of the position and the program, Ellie felt herself getting enthused, a feeling she hadn't had in the last few years. Impulsively, she said, "Dave, you've sold me on this program and the job. I'll take it."

Dave's look was one of pleasure because he'd finally filled the hard to hire job of teacher/director for his adult ed program. Additionally, he felt he'd made a real find because Ellie's qualifications were so far ahead of everyone he'd interviewed previously. He knew he was rushing things because he hadn't even checked her references but barring a criminal record, which he highly doubted, he wanted Ellie for the job. Most of the applicants didn't know about the curriculum in adult education, GED prep or ESL, let alone have any experience.

Ellie drove home to her empty house and Duke, who dutifully listened when she told him all about her interview and her new job. She wished she had someone nearby to share her news with, but all her friends were back in upstate New York and working at their jobs. She decided she'd call her Auntie Flo in Colorado to tell her about the job because she was retired now and wouldn't be interrupted at work by Ellie's call.

"Auntie Flo? Did I get you at a bad time?" Ellie asked her godmother and honorary aunt.

"No, dear, this is a good time, but it is unusual for you to call me mid-week during my nap time. Before you apologize and hang up, let me reassure you that I was awake and took an early nap today," Flo said with a laugh.

"Good! I'm just flustered, I guess. I got this wild hair up my you know where today to go ahead and look for a summer school job and I got called almost right after I submitted the application online. Isn't the internet wonderful? This would have taken weeks in the old days, wouldn't it? So, I went in and didn't get the job I applied for but got another at twice the pay that's a combo director and teacher position. I'll be the administrator plus teach a few classes. I'm actually excited though I did think this was all moving kind of fast."

"Congratulations! I'm glad you're getting off your rear and doing something other than tend your herb garden and talk to that dog of yours," Flo told Ellie seriously.

"Oh, well. Don't hold back, Auntie Flo. Was it that bad?"

"Do you even have to ask, child?" Flo responded.

"Now I'm 'child' again. I guess it looked different from the outside looking in than it did to me just sitting around here. I thought that moving back to Texas was a big positive step. I forgot to think much further though and hadn't really done much since I'd been back," Ellie said and had to admit that Flo had a point. Now that she'd stepped out of her comfort zone, she saw how limited her life had become. Back in upstate New York, she had kept up with her friends and her volunteer projects, but since she'd been back, she'd made no effort to reconnect with her old Texas friends or to get involved locally doing some volunteer work which she really used to enjoy..

"Well, Ellie. I'm happy for you and I think your new job is going to open lots of doors for you. Thanks for calling and letting me in on your news," Flo said, her smile in her voice.

"Thanks, Auntie Flo. I just had to share it with you. I'll keep you updated better this time about what's going on. Take care. Love you, bye."

Hearing some excitement in her voice, Duke got up and came over to put his head on Ellie's knee, giving her what she interpreted as an encouraging look. *'Crap. Even my dog's excited I'm getting up off my ass and doing something. It's pathetic when your dog wants something more for his owner. He must be really bored to even care.'*

'Tomorrow's a big day for me. It's been more than three years since I've worked, and this is a return to my early years of working when I was a classroom teacher plus, I'm going to run the program. I'm glad the salary's good for all that I'm going to have to do.'

"Well, Duke. Bedtime. Let's get a good night's sleep. Outside for you though for one last potty run," Ellie said as Duke jumped up when he heard her say 'outside.'

Chapter 2: Back at the New Job

Ellie jumped right into her new job in the morning after Dave showed her to where her office would be located and where the classrooms were, conveniently located not too far away. She mentally groaned when she saw the unorganized mess left in her office and looked questioningly at Dave.

"Er, ahem. Yes, this place needs some work. I'd like to tell you to just toss everything, but unfortunately, curriculum guides and old lessons plans are stuck in the midst of this mess, and I think you should see what we've been doing previously. Hopefully there's some useful resources here buried under this debris. Today, you can try to bring some order to this office and tomorrow you'll meet your staff. They will have one day of prep and then students will arrive on Monday. Good luck," Dave said ruefully and turned to leave.

'Crap! No wonder this program needs a new director. I just hope I can find some curriculum guides and lesson plans. I'd hate to have to create everything from scratch in two days plus a weekend,' Ellie thought and sighed as she dug into the first teetering stack of papers.

Dave came by around 12:30 and seemed surprised to see Ellie sitting on the floor surrounded by neat stacks of paper. It was actually possible to walk into the office without feeling like he was walking through a hoarder's house.

"Ellie! Have you had lunch? I came to collect you to get you out of here if you haven't."

"Uh, no, Dave. I've been busy as you can see, but I am starting to find some promising things. I forgot to ask, is there a secretary for our program? I don't want prospective students trying to call in without reaching anyone."

"Well, that's something we hadn't really thought of. Come with me and we can talk about it at lunch. OK?"

Sitting in the junior college cafeteria a little while later, Ellie said, "If there's no money for a secretary, can we assign a student worker or intern to cover phones at least part of the day? When I worked for Mohican College, we had a pool of student workers on scholarships that got paid stipends by the college for their jobs and they helped out all around campus. We need our number and voicemail set up also. Can you make this happen? Oh, one more thing: being bilingual Spanish/English would be a real help."

"I can appreciate your thinking like an administrator Ellie. No one has in this program for quite a while. Good suggestions, especially about the student worker."

"My first adult education job was run under a federally funded grant by a university in Ohio and money was always an issue, so we had to be creative in finding ways to meet our needs at minimal cost. I never realized that public school programs were lucky to have so much more provided until I worked as an English as a Second Language teacher in public school and was amazed that I could get basic necessities for our students without having to do car washes and raffles. Ha!"

"Well, I think it's too soon to see our new director having to do a car wash, so I'll get on what you just asked me. Is there anything else concerning you?"

"That's it for now. Thanks, Dave. I'll see you later."

Ellie planned to go over some of her lists for the books and classroom needs and returned to her office after lunch to get after the rest of the mess still to be sorted through. About five minutes after she returned, she heard someone clearing his throat and then a knock at the door. Looking up, Ellie was surprised to see a good-looking man about her age or a little younger standing in her doorway.

"Yes. Can I help you?" Ellie asked with a smile.

"Er, yes you can. I'm the custodian in this area and I see you have a lot of clutter. The fact that you're sitting in it makes me think it's not all trash. Yes?"

"No, it's not. At least most of it's not," Ellie replied and got to her feet to go over to meet her visitor.

"Hi, Ellie Thompson. Nice to meet you," she said and extended her hand.

Looking surprised, the custodian looked at her for a moment and then put his hand in hers. "Noé Vasquez."

"Oh, Mr. Vasquez. You're not from around here are you?"

Not sure whether to be offended or curious, Noe said, "Why do you say that, Ms. Thompson?"

"Oh, I'm sorry if that sounded too personal. I knew you came from somewhere else by your handshake. I teach Adult Basic Education and English as a Second Language and that's one of the units that I teach: the American handshake."

"Now I have to ask, what's wrong with my handshake?"

"Nothing. Nothing's wrong with it. It's just not American. That may be something you want to learn or not depending on what your career goals are."

"Career goals? Maybe you forgot to notice that I'm a custodian. What kind of career goals would you expect me to have?" Noé said with some bitterness and a little annoyance.

"I can't catch a break here today it seems. I said that because while you are a custodian here, you are very well spoken and clearly educated. Hence my assumption that you might have other career goals. Pardon my intrusion into your life and your day," Ellie said, also annoyed at the turn their conversation was taking.

Giving Ellie a long, measuring look, Noé nodded and turned to leave saying over his shoulder, "You might make a good detective, Ms. Thompson."

'Grrr. If he weren't so good looking, I'd be pissed at that man. I guess he can have a pass this time. I probably sounded too nosy anyway. It's something I tend to do when a situation overlaps with my teaching field. Note to self: stop meddling and giving unsolicited advice,' Ellie told herself ruefully.

The day flew by, and Ellie was surprised when Dave appeared at her door again and said, "Wow! This is some transformation. I can hardly believe you could make order out of this mess. It's been months in the making, and no one was brave enough to tackle it."

"Thanks, Dave, but it was either sink or swim. If I didn't get it under control, I'd never have a place to work and meet with students, let alone manage to locate curriculum guides. It was a very productive day. The best part was finding guides for computer software to individualize instruction. I had no idea we'd have that resource available," Looking up at the clock over her door, Ellie was surprised to see that it was after 5:00. "Geez! The day really went fast. Time to go home."

"See you tomorrow, Ellie. Your staff will be in at 9, so you can come in late tomorrow. You've more than put in a full day today. For all this work, I'd give you the day off tomorrow, except I can't. Sorry," Dave said ruefully.

Laughing, Ellie said, "No problem, Dave. I'm on a roll and can't wait to whip this all into shape. There's still a lot of work to be done. See you."

Walking to her car, Ellie noticed parking stickers on windshields of cars still left in the lot and made a mental note to herself to check on getting her sticker tomorrow and finding out where she was supposed to park. As she rounded the last building, she jumped and squealed when someone stepped out and started walking beside her."

"Geez! Mr. Vasquez, you just gave me a heart attack. No, don't look at me like that. Clearly you didn't give me a heart attack. I like hyperbole. I mean that you scared the crap out of me. No, not literally. I sound like I'm twelve. Pardon me and forget everything I'm saying. I'm too tired to be coherent."

Putting his hands up in front of him, Noé smiled, "No, excuse me. I didn't mean to terrify you. I just wanted to be sure you got to your car with no problem because campus security isn't on the job patrolling the parking lots till Monday."

Touched by his thoughtfulness, Ellie said, "Why, Mr. Vasquez, that's very kind of you. I appreciate your thoughtfulness." Ellie, who had been walking while they were talking, quickly arrived at her car and unlocked the door.

"No problem. Oh, by the way, Mexico City," Noé said, turned and started to walk away.

Laughing, Ellie got in her car and said, "Mexico City? Why that's one of my favorite places." She still remembered the good times she'd had there spending winter quarter in Mexico her sophomore year in college. "Small world."

The next day, Ellie came in at eight to get after the work remaining to develop curriculum before Monday and was surprised when someone knocked on her door at nine. The time had flown by again. One thing was certain, she wasn't bored on this job. She was too busy. Smiling, she looked at the two people at her door expectantly.

"Er, hello. I'm Trace and this is Courtney. We're the new teachers in the adult education program. Mr. Morris sent us over to meet you."

"Yes. It's nice to meet you both. I'm Ellie Thompson, also a teacher in the program as well as the director. Let's get started in the conference room. Do you need anything before we go there? I have a Keurig over there on the counter if you want to get yourselves a cup of coffee to take along. Mugs are in the cupboard above. We're a long way from the main staff lounge, so I guess we'll learn to fend for ourselves."

Trace and Courtney looked at her for a minute and then both went to get a cup of coffee.

'Egads. I feel like I'm a doddering old woman next to these two. They don't look old enough to have graduated from college, so I'm guessing they don't have any experience. Oh well. They'll learn how to be teachers here.'

Arriving in the conference room, Ellie said, "I want us to introduce ourselves and I'll start by saying that I did my undergrad work at the Ohio State University and my first master's program at HBU in Houston and also the educational leadership master's program at U of H in Sugar Land though the program was part of the Victoria campus then. I first taught in public school in Ohio: high school Spanish and English. Next, I taught in an adult ed program also in Ohio where I taught GED prep, math, ESL and Spanish literature to students who took the GED in Spanish. I came to Texas and taught high school Spanish, English, and ESL in grades K through 12; then became a high school assistant principal. My last job was for a private college in upstate New York where I was the academic coordinator in an at-risk dropout prevention program. And now I'm here getting back into things."

Trace and Courtney looked uncomfortable until Ellie said, "Do you need me to tell you who goes first?"

"Er, no. I'll go first. I graduated from Needville and then went here for my first two years of college and then finished up in Victoria. I tutored English all through college and my major is English with a minor in social studies," Trace said and looked up to see Ellie's reaction.

"Great. I like your experience, Trace. That will be helpful here. I taught in Needville when I first came to Texas but not when you were most likely there. Courtney, what do you want to do for your career?"

"I don't know. I guess that's why I'm here. I couldn't find anything else, and my parents wanted me to try this to see if I liked teaching."

"Great, Courtney. Trace, what are your career objectives? Do you plan on teaching? Do you want to be a writer?"

Surprised, Trace asked, "Why would you ask that? How did you know?"

"English majors often have an interest in writing and enjoy all that literature they have to read for their degrees. I was an English minor in college for that same reason. The problem with writing is finding a way to make it pay for a decent living, isn't that the case?"

"Yes. I wish you could tell my parents that there can be something worthwhile coming out of my degree. They think they've wasted their money," Trace said dejectedly.

"Yours think you've wasted your time and their money; try explaining art history to them!" Courtney interjected and added, "I went to school in Katy and went to college at Trinity University and majored in art history," Courtney said and then also looked at Ellie for her reaction.

"Sounds like we have social studies and English coursework backgrounds which gives us a starting point. Well, you're both here now and I will help you figure out if teaching has any interest for you. It could be the career that pays your bills while you figure out a way to make your first academic interests pay. We will work together on planning and you're welcome to watch me teach a few classes while you're getting your students settled in to get the hang of what to do. Does that help make you less concerned about how you're going to handle this job?" Ellie said to reassure her new recruits who were looking decidedly worried.

"Yes! Thank you!" they both responded with a much less worried look on their faces.

The morning went quickly as Ellie went over the curriculum guides and showed Trace and Courtney how to create lesson plans with weekly goals. She told them that some of what they did would feel like tutoring because most of their students wouldn't be on the same level as anyone else and in those situations, it would feel like a one room schoolhouse from days in the past. She also showed them the computer room between her classroom and Courtney's and said to be sure to include computer time when it fit in with their lessons. They could develop a schedule for the lab as they got to know their students.

Around noon, Trace and Courtney asked if they could go eat lunch and Ellie told them to come back by one and they'd start up again. She watched them hurry away as if they were glad to escape for a while. On their heels, Dave turned up again and knocked.

"How'd it go? I saw our new recruits almost running to get away from here. Did you terrify them this morning? Come on, let's walk and talk at the same time and head over to the Commons to eat. OK?"

"Dave, I don't know when I've seen greener recruits. Most new teachers have at least done student teaching and have some interest in being teachers. These two took these jobs as a last resort to pacify their parents. I hope they last out the week," Ellie said and sighed.

By then they'd arrived at the cafeteria called the Commons and went in and through the line. Taking her tray to the closest table, Ellie sat down and looked over at Dave who was smiling ruefully.

"OK. Spill it. Why that look?"

"I was desperate when these two showed up at my office the same day at different times. I'd given up finding anyone to fill these two positions. Living and breathing with any kind of college degree was all I was looking for at that point. I share your concerns and hope they last. They didn't look especially hardy and adventurous, did they?

"Adventurous?! You're kidding. Terrified would be the best descriptor. Oh, I meant to ask you before and forgot till I got back to my list of 'to do's' whether we have any volunteers to use as tutors? Sometimes students and community members just want to do a good thing. High school seniors who are 17, which is most of them, could tutor for community service hours and maybe I can speak with some of the local church groups to see if there are any members who'd like to help out in their community. Would that be alright? Is there any college policy against that here?

"Not that I know of, but I'll ask legal before I give you the OK. As long as they'd be supervised and in the room with one of the teachers or you, I don't have a problem with it and think it's actually a great idea. How'd you come up with that one?"

"The last time I taught high school ESL, a parent at the rich high school where I was teaching approached the principal at open house and said she'd like to volunteer in ESL classes if there was a need, that she had time on her hands and wanted to do something useful. The principal gave me her number which I promptly called. She ended up coming in twice and week and I gave her a group of beginners to tutor in reading. It's funny because a couple of years later, I worked as a district level administrator in ESL and recruited her as an ESL teacher for an elementary school under my supervision. She was amazing and the nicest lady. I've had good luck with teacher's aides and volunteers and don't see a reason not to give it a try here unless you have objections."

"Tentative 'yes' till I ask legal. I personally think it's a great idea. Now tell me how it went with your two newbies."

"Once I decided that they weren't high school escapees and that they were really old enough to be college graduates, I think I intimidated them when I gave them the run down on my experience. Once I heard about their non-experience, I could see why they were afraid to share. Trace at least, has experience tutoring which he did throughout his college years. That should serve him well.

I'm a little worried about Courtney though as she's a bit of a timid mouse. I hope our students don't turn out to be too hard core for her. She's so young she may not be able to see beyond first impressions. I'll have to watch her closely. We'll start slowly and I want them to watch me teach a few classes to get some ideas about what to do. It's hard to communicate all that's involved in a few days.

We've made some real progress with curriculum planning and how to set weekly goals in lesson plans along with objectives, outcomes and measures of success. At this point, I'd love it if we could find some tutors here who want to go into education. They could prove invaluable and probably have as many or more skills as our new teachers."

"At the risk of flattering you too much so that you want a raise, which I can't give you, you really are impressive, Ellie. I feel good about where we're going to go with this program. This is the first time it hasn't seemed like a hopeless mess that just had no solution, at least not one I could think of. Thank you!"

Ellie smiled at Dave and looked up as she saw Noé pass by their table carrying a lunch box and a drink. "Mr. Vasquez come over and join us if you'd like," Ellie said but then noticed Dave's look of surprise.

"No. No thank you, Ms. Thompson," Noé said looking uncomfortably at Dave and walking past to a table over in the corner.

"What was that about? How do you know the custodian? I admit I was shocked when you invited him to sit here with us," Dave said and looked at Ellie questioningly.

"I met Mr. Vasquez when he came by to pick up some of the piles of trash from my office. Is it a problem to mix with the staff? Is the service staff expected to go sit by themselves in the corner over there?" Ellie asked with disapproval in her voice.

"Hold on a minute, Ellie. I didn't say that. It sounds like you're critical of how it's always done here. There's nothing wrong with them having their own area to eat. After all, they are in the same cafeteria with the rest of us."

"Well, Dave, we'll have to disagree on that one. You are aware that Texas had segregated schools before they were forced to segregate, yes? Also, in south Texas, signs on water fountains said, 'No dogs or Mexicans.' Somehow class distinctions at a place of higher learning seem contrary to what a college is all about," Ellie said stiffly and resumed eating.

"Jesus, Ellie, let's not fight. I'm sorry I said anything. You're right. If Mr. Vasquez wants to sit here next time, it'll be fine with me. I think you're going to keep me on my toes, Ellie. You are right," Dave said with a sigh.

Back in her office after lunch, Ellie started watching the clock when one came and went without a sign of Trace and Courtney. She decided to go to the conference room in case they'd gone straight there but found no one waiting. Finally, at 1:15, they ran into the conference room, out of breath and looking guilty.

"Since we're barely started, I won't hold today against either of you, but it does tell me that I may have to be concerned about your promptness in the future. One thing a teacher cannot be is late. **Never**. We'll forget today, but the next time, I will give you a verbal warning which I will document. After that, it's a written warning. I will talk to personnel about the paper trail required to fire you if you continue to disregard my rules about time on the job. Is that clear?" Ellie said with a frown and got out her I-Pad and made a note.

Looking defiant, Trace said, "I think you're making a big deal out of this, Ms. Thompson. We weren't that late."

"Don't bother, Trace. It **is** a big deal. It's bad enough that you disregarded my instructions; now you're whining and trying to minimize the situation rather than taking responsibility for your screw up. Understand that this is a big deal to me and any administrator in school or business and let's move on to someone more productive. We have a lot to do to get ready for our students. Agreed?" Ellie said and looked at Trace and Courtney to see if they had more to say. However, her expression said, 'shut the hell up.'

Courtney wouldn't make eye contact and looked miserable, and Trace finally knew it was time to shut his mouth, so he nodded and reached for his lesson planning notebook and realized that what he'd thought was going to be a job he could coast through had taken a drastic turn in another direction but tried to wipe the sour look off his face so Ellie wouldn't say anything else to him.

At five, Ellie said, "All right. Today's been very productive. Meet me back here at 9 a.m. and we'll get the rest of what we'll need for Monday's first day prepared. Questions?"

"No. See you tomorrow," Trace said as he got up. Courtney just followed suit silently and they quickly exited.

Ellie gathered up the materials and then locked the door and returned to her office to find Dave waiting here at her doorway.

"Well, did they get any better during the afternoon?" Dave asked.

"Once I got through chewing them out for being fifteen minutes late coming back from lunch, we got a lot done. I need to talk with you about Human Resources' procedures to document employee problems. Not knowing what they would be, I told them I'd let today slide, but the next time, I would give them a verbal warning which I would document and then next would come a written warning. How does that sound?"

Dave groaned, "Jesus, I'd hoped they'd get off to a better start than that. I'll check with HR legal to be sure, but what you said sounds right. It seems too early to be looking at creating an improvement plan for new hires."

"Courtney was horrified, and I don't think she'll cause more problems, but Trace was defiant and whiney. I told him to stop whining and get to work. I'm sure he's still complaining to himself about it. He's very immature."

"Well, I'll check in with you tomorrow in the afternoon. I have meetings all morning, a lunch meeting and then another meeting after that. I also oversee some curricular committees. It seems like everyone has some last-minute detail they need to get resolved."

"OK, Dave. See you tomorrow. Don't worry about us. We'll be ready," Ellie said as she was putting things away on the top of the desk and the bookshelf behind her chair. Shortly after, she heard a knock at her door and looked up to see Noé at her door.

"Hi, Noé, or I guess I mean Mr. Vasquez though I'm perfectly fine with first names. How are you this evening?"

"Hello, Ms. Thompson. I'm fine and you may call me Noé if you like though not in front of the students or other staff."

"Oh, dear, more rules that I'll probably forget. Was that what happened at lunch today? I wondered why you wouldn't sit down at my table."

Noé rolled his eyes and said, "Ellie, did you see the look on your boss's face when you said that? What you asked just isn't done here."

"You mean men and women eating lunch together? Dave, a man, was already sitting there so that shouldn't have been the problem."

"Are you new to Texas? Things don't work like that in this town. That's the problem."

"Things like that. OK, let me be helpful and say, staff and professional people eating together is some sort of taboo here. Is that what you're trying to tell me without actually saying the words?"

Relieved that Ellie did understand at least part of it, Noé nodded and smiled.

"But, Noé, that's a bunch of crap and I told that to Dave and he reluctantly agreed though I have to admit that he didn't seem happy. I said that I was surprised to hear about those kinds of attitudes at an institution of higher learning. I think I shamed him into agreeing, but what the hell."

Taken aback, Noé laughed and said, "You're going to be butting heads with a lot of people around here with those ideas."

"Well, it's something I'm used to in rural Texas. When I first came to Texas years ago to teach, I found the same old prejudiced ideas everywhere. It felt more like the 50's instead of the 90's. It was hard, but now we're more than twenty years later and I just can't accept those old ideas. I won't put up with that racist, prejudiced shit. Excuse my language, Noé. It seems like I can't say much without surprising or more exactly, horrifying you. Sorry."

"Quite the opposite. It's refreshing, Ellie. I'm glad you're here. Some people need a little shaking up around here."

"Don't get me wrong, Noé. I'm not on some campaign to change the racism here, but in my own little world, I won't tolerate that around me if I can change it. Now, back to the cafeteria. Would it bother you to eat lunch with me?"

"No, I'd be honored, but I think for a while, I need to stick with my guys for now. I'd spend all my time explaining to them what I was doing eating lunch with a white woman, a *gringa*."

"Got it," Ellie said and grimaced but finished with a smile. "Now, I'm ready to go home. Did you come to be sure I was safe on the way to the parking lot again?"

"Yes, I did and since I terrified you yesterday by waiting out behind a building, I thought it'd be less threatening to you if I came to your office. Yes?"

"Definitely. After the day I've had, I don't think I could have survived another fright. It's very kind of you to walk with me. I really do appreciate it. Thank you, Noé," Ellie said and smiled at him as she picked up her briefcase and purse.

"Here, let me carry your briefcase for you," Noé said as he took her briefcase out of her hand.

"Geez, Noé, no one's done that for me since high school. Thanks," Ellie said and laughed.

"Well, someone should have. I'm pleased I can help you. Think of it as a way to thank you for the lunch invitation which was a bold move around this campus."

Chapter 3: Auntie Flo

When Ellie got home from work, she was surprised to see her Aunt Flo's car parked in her driveway. *'Did I miss something? I don't remember talking about a visit from my favorite aunt.'*

Getting out of her car, Ellie ran up to Flo who apparently had just gotten out of her car as she was trying to get her suitcase out of the back seat and gave her a big hug. "Did I miss something in our conversation Flo? Oh, no, now I've got Alzheimer's to deal with on top of everything else. I'm too young and just too busy for a change for that complication at this time of my life."

Laughing, Flo returned the hug and turned to pull her suitcase out of the back seat of her car. "You didn't know. I'm a complete surprise and I can tell from the look on your face that I am a surprise that could be a good one. You don't look horrified at least. Come on, let's go inside. It's too hot to stand out here in this God-awful heat."

Sitting inside the cool house, they each sat at the kitchen table with a big glass of iced tea.

"This is good, Ellie. Is that mint from your herb garden? I'll bet it is. You always did have a way with plants. I can't tell you who you got that from in our family though because none of us could keep even a house plant alive."

"Oh, Flo. Yes, it is from my little herb garden, and I'll take you out back to show you the extent of my gardening projects later this evening when it cools down a little. It's almost June and it's just getting hot. You know it'll get much worse this summer. I'm bracing myself for the long, grueling summer. I've been spoiled in upstate New York those years where summers are wonderful."

"Yeah, but winter's a bitch there. You've got to admit that," Ellie said laughing as she took another sip of tea. "You've got to admit that if the cold doesn't bother you, the snow and roads closed for bad weather are huge up there."

"OK, Auntie Flo. Now are you going to tell me why you came down here unexpectedly? You had to drive all night or get up beyond early. It's a thirteen-hour trip from Trinidad, Colorado to here. That's a long way to drive alone. What possessed you to do this?"

"I heard something in your voice when I talked to you and just felt that here was where I needed to be. I had my satellite radio to keep me company though people on the road with me probably thought me odd as I was belting out the tunes along with the radio. Back to the 'why.' After all, Duke will be lonely come Monday when you're not here with him during the day, right Duke?" Flo said and patted Duke's head.

"Yes, Flo, but Duke will adjust. He always does. It's time for me to get going with my life again. I'm not sick. I got through all of that. I'm no longer in exile in New York as you liked to call my time up there and I think I'm going to really like my new job. I haven't met any students yet, though, so that may all change Monday after I see my first students. It's been years since I taught in adult ed, but it was my all-time favorite job, so I'm really glad I found a combination of administrator and teacher job. It even pays well too. I'm looking forward to it. There, does that make you feel better?"

"It does, honey. I'm glad for you. You needed to get unstuck and talk to someone other than your dog. You haven't joined a church or any local service clubs, have you? I can see by your face that you haven't. Hibernation time was due to end, overdue."

Feeling guilty and not a little self-indulgent, Ellie nodded in agreement. "I just couldn't seem to get myself motivated in my little cocoon in upstate New York. You know I loved it there, but it wasn't really reality anymore. I knew I'd never get going if I stayed there, so that's why I moved back here. Duke hates it though with this heat and humidity and I now remember how much I hated the heat."

"That's why you have air-conditioning. Don't tell me your car doesn't have A/C!"

Laughing at her aunt's shocked expression, Ellie said, "Yes, Flo. I have A/C. Duke's decided he's an inside dog now though for summer and my car thankfully does have A/C. I would have traded it for another if it didn't. It's too hot and humid here to mess around. Oh, remind me to get a new sunshade for my windshield, Auntie Flo. We're going to survive this heat, I imagine, though I don't think I'll be able to stop complaining about it just yet."

"Well, good. That's what I hoped you'd say, though I can't say I'm looking forward to your complaining. You hate whining and always have; complaining and whining walk a fine line of distinction. Remember that," Flo admonished with a smile.

"Now, tell me about the new people you've met at work already. Surely there are a few interesting people, though I expect you'll have more to say when your students start arriving."

"Starting with my boss, Dave Morris, he's the first person I've met here and he's about fifteen to twenty years younger than I am. At first, I wasn't sure if I'd like him, but I think I intimidate him a little. The good thing is that he seems to genuinely care about the adult ed program. However, we had a disagreement at lunch and I more or less shamed him into agreeing with me."

"Oh, that sounds interesting! What did you disagree over? Tell me the details."

"Auntie Flo, you sound like a gossip," Ellie said reprovingly.

"Yes, of course, I do. This **is** gossip. Now get back to your story, girl."

"I invited the custodian to eat at our table with us and my boss took issue after the custodian had refused and walked to another table. The custodian knew he wasn't welcome and walked on, but I was pissed. I couldn't decide if it was a racist thing or a social class thing with Dave," Ellie explained seriously remembering the incident.

"Was the custodian not white?" Flo asked with interest.

"He wasn't Black, but he was Hispanic and in this part of Texas, that's the same thing: the wrong color."

"I guess my next question should be how you met this Hispanic custodian you wanted to be your lunch companion?"

"I met him when he came by my office the first day to ask if I wanted all the trash I'd gone through taken away or if it had any meaningful purpose. Oh, and then he waited outside one of the buildings to walk me to my car in the parking lot after work because security on campus didn't start till Monday and he didn't want me to walk alone. Very gentlemanly," Ellie explained.

"Yes, that is gentlemanly. Or it could be that he's hitting on you at the same time he's keeping you safe. Have you thought about that?" Flo asked with interest.

"What? Oh, no. Why would you think that?"

"Ellie, you might have forgotten, but you're an attractive woman and you're still at an age where men would notice you. Why wouldn't he be flirting a little with you?" Flo demanded.

"Geez, I don't know, Auntie Flo. Maybe because I am getting grey hairs in my hair around my face, my body is starting to show the effects of gravity and I'm a boring schoolteacher," Ellie responded with disgust as she pulled her hair back from her face so Flo could better see her grey hairs.

"Don't worry about a little grey, dear. If you don't like it, go to the beauty salon and have them take care of it. Frost it, streak it or something if you don't want to change all the color to another shade. You're in good shape and you have a wicked sense of humor. At the risk of sounding repetitive, why wouldn't he be flirting with you? If I were a man, I would," Flo said and crossed her arms with a defiant look on her face.

"Oh, Flo, you do make me laugh. Thank you. That's just what I needed after an exasperating day. Come on, let's go into the living room and catch the national news. I finally got my DISH satellite installed so I can record the shows I want to catch up on later, like the local and national news. I know you drove eight hundred and fifty miles to watch the news with me. Not! But I do want to catch the weather without staying up late to watch. I'm really tired today and want to go to bed early. I must be at work a little before eight tomorrow morning. It should be a big day as it's the last day before our students arrive. I've got to be sure my teachers are prepared with their lesson plans and I also need to give them a crash course in cultural awareness, so they realize who adult students often are in programs like ours."

"Sounds good. Oh, I heard the doorbell. That's the pizza I ordered while I was waiting for you to come home. I didn't think either of us would be energetic enough to cook tonight or bother to go out to eat," Flo said as she got up to go to the door.

"Oh, Flo, thank you! That's perfect. Good thing we like the same kind of pizza. Now that you mention it, I am hungry."

Later, a few pieces of the pizza left on the table between them, Flo asked, "So, now that we're recharged, tell me about your custodian."

"**My** custodian? I think you're getting ahead of yourself here. He's just a new friend I've only known for several days. All I know about him is that while he has a strong accent, he sounds very well educated from his grammar and vocabulary proficiency. Oh, and he told me he's from Mexico City."

"I see you do know more about him than you were letting on. You've done your language analysis of him and know where he's from. That's a good start. Now, tell me what he looks like, if he's good looking," Flo continued looking eager for details.

"Argh. I can see there's no stopping you till you've extracted all I know about him. Yes, I would say he's good looking. He's about my height though definitely a little taller by a few inches. He's trim and looks like he works out some though that could be from his custodial work. I don't really know how long he's been at the junior college though. His hair is black with some distinguished grey at the temples and he's clean shaven. Is that enough detail for you?"

"Perfect. He sounds like the perfect candidate to get you back into the social scene. I wonder if he likes to dance."

"It sounds like he'd be more to your liking, Auntie Flo if you're going there with the dancing interest. Maybe I should introduce him to you. You're not that much older than I am. You were a young aunt, right?"

"Now who's getting ahead of herself? And I'm not looking. You know I keep myself quite busy with my clubs and volunteer work back home. I don't have the time to come down here to find a boyfriend, thank you very much," Flo said and laughed as she tossed her hair.

"Oh, Flo. I really don't have the time or the inclination to find someone to date now. I'm just starting a new job that sounds like it will be challenging while I get things organized and on the right track. Thanks for your concern about my disappointing love life, but now's just not the time. I'll let you know when things change, alright?"

"Deal. Now, let's catch up on the news and weather and then maybe find something to watch on TV before we go to bed. I'll admit that I am tired and want to make an early night of it. At least the news and programs are on an hour earlier here since we're in the central time zone rather than the eastern zone you've been used to these past few years."

"Thank you, Auntie Flo for being in my life and coming down here to my rescue though I really didn't think I was that in need of rescue. I love that you dropped everything and came down to see for yourself that I was doing well. You're still the best."

The next morning, Ellie woke to the smell of coffee and pancakes as she rolled over when Duke put his cold nose on her cheek to wake her. Groaning, she looked at the clock and was relieved to see that it was only six thirty and she had plenty of time to eat and shower and still get to work on time. Giving Duke a pat, Ellie got up and wandered to the kitchen after a pit stop at her ensuite bathroom, one of the features she really liked about her comfy little home. It was so convenient in so many ways that Ellie felt fortunate to have found it when she needed it.

"Good morning. I probably woke you up, but that was the whole idea, right?" Flo said with a smile as she handed Ellie a cup of coffee. This tastes as good as it smells. I brought some of that new organic Colorado coffee with me to give it a try. So far, so good as far as I'm concerned. It's a big agricultural experiment there because they need to take care of the tender beans as it's a little colder where they're growing this coffee than is traditionally done. It's mostly Kentucky coffee they've been successful with though that tastes like a combo of old coffee and whiskey. What do you think, El?"

"I like it. It smells heavenly and tastes great. How 'bout some of those pancakes I smelled when I got up?"

"Here you go. I knew that they would get your attention if the coffee failed to do its job to wake you up. Mission accomplished. Yeah!" Flo said laughingly as she brought the stack of pancakes over to the table from the warming oven. Next, she set the bottle of maple syrup on the table in front of Ellie and waited for her response."

Ellie didn't notice the expectant look on Flo's face and dug into her pancakes after drenching them with the warm maple syrup. "Oh, these are sooo good! And this syrup is divine," Ellie said as she turned the jug around and saw that it was from Clinton, New York, and was her favorite from a farm not far from hers where she'd lived in upstate. "Oh, Flo, it's Shaw's maple syrup. My favorite. Thank you!" Ellie said and got up to walk around the table to give her aunt Flo a hug.

"I thought you'd get a kick out of tasting something from home plus they make really good maple syrup. Ever since you took me to their little farm store and I stocked up, I've been using their syrup. I just order it online though. It's a twenty-six-hour drive to Clinton from Trinidad, so I don't even pretend that's a trip I can easily make. Plus no matter how good that syrup is, I'm not going to drive that far to get it. Online is a gift to me."

"Auntie Flo, you're the best. Thank you," Ellie said as tears welled up in her eyes.

"Now, no time for tears. You know I like to spoil you when I get the chance, and it was time for a little treat. Pull yourself together and go take that shower. I'll let Duke outside in the back yard, so don't worry about him."

Hearing his name and the word "outside", Duke got up and came over to stand beside Flo with an expectant look on his face, his ears perked up. "Yes, Duke, I said your name. Let's you and I go outside for that morning back yard visit while El gets ready for work. It's you and me today anyway, so let's get started. Duke woofed at Flo and looked hopefully toward the door, woofing again when Flo moved towards the back door to let him out.

Hurrying through her shower, not bothering to wash her hair, pinning it up on top of her head so she could shorten her shower time and get dressed, Ellie mentally ran through what she needed to get done once she got to work. She thought she'd start with her parking sticker and then go to her office. *'Yes, that'll work. I can at least find out about the parking before I get immersed in all I want to get done. There's that little cultural awareness talk I want to give my newbies too. That shouldn't take that long. I wish I had some visuals to show them to condition their inexperienced brains not to judge a book by its cover.'* Turning off the shower, Ellie quickly dried off, brushed her teeth, put on sunscreen and got dressed.

"Here's a breakfast sandwich to go, dear. It's an English muffin with ham, eggs, and a slice of cheese. Those pancakes won't stay with you all morning till lunch. That's for one hand and this mug of coffee is for the other," Flo said as she handed Ellie her breakfast and coffee and hurried her toward the door.

"Auntie Flo, once again, you're the best. I certainly wouldn't have gotten anything for breakfast and probably wouldn't have even gotten coffee. This is great! Thank you," Ellie said as she hugged Flo, careful not to spill her coffee. "Bye, Duke. See you both later."

By the time Ellie had gotten to campus, she'd managed to eat a few bites of her sandwich without dropping anything on her clothes and even take a few sips of her coffee. Feeling better, she parked and quickly went to her office where she set down her sandwich and coffee and then locked up again and went to the administration building to find information on her parking sticker and where she really should be parking come Monday.

A half hour later, Ellie made her way back to her office and unlocked and went in to sit at her desk so she could finish her sandwich and get some fresh coffee. She was just sitting down again when she heard a knock at her door. "Yes, can I help . . .? Oh, Noé, how are you today? Would you like to get a cup of coffee? There are some extra mugs in the cupboard above the Keurig."

"Why, thanks, Ellie. That's very nice, but I think a custodian hanging out here drinking your coffee would be frowned upon by just about everyone. I don't want to keep you because I know your new teachers will be here within an hour and you'll be busy. I just wanted to stop by and say 'hi,' and ask you if you have plans for tomorrow night?"

Blushing, Ellie swallowed and said, "Tomorrow night? Why, Noé?"

Smiling and hesitating as if gathering his courage, Noé said, "I want to invite you to go with me to an outdoor concert and rodeo near here. Will you go with me?"

"Noe, that sounds like fun. I'd like to. How fancy is this? I'm thinking outdoor means casual. Women need to ask these questions to satisfy our obsession with proper attire if you were wondering why I'm even asking. But no, you probably weren't wondering because you're a guy and guys don't bother with that kind of trivia. OK. I'll stop talking now," Ellie said as she saw a slow smile light up Noé's face.

"Yes, casual and when I walk you to your car later today, you will tell me where you live so I can pick you up. I'll do that around six-thirty tomorrow night if that's alright with you."

"Yes. I'll see you later and we can talk then. You're right about the time though because I see that my new teachers should be here in fifteen minutes and I need to get my head wrapped around what I'm going to indoctrinate them with. I spent an entire half hour this morning trying to get a parking sticker and still have to go back there this afternoon to get that finally taken care of. At least I know where to send my new teachers now, but I'll admit I didn't expect something so simple to be so complicated. I guess that's bureaucracy. Oh well. Bye now," Ellie said as Noé smiled again and turned to go.

'It's clearly been too long since I've been on a date. I was babbling there for a minute. Just because a handsome guy asks me out doesn't mean I need to become a bumbling,

witless fool in a matter of seconds. I feel like a youngster again and I can't say that I like it. Note to self, calm down when Noé's around so you don't scare him away.'

Promptly at eight, Courtney and Trace walked into her office and Ellie said, "Good morning, you two. If you'd like, get yourselves a cup of coffee and we'll go over to the conference room and get started. It's our last prep day before classes and we have a lot to do. I hope that later in the day, they'll have our class rosters ready so we can know how many students to plan for."

Not having much to say, Courtney and Trace just followed Ellie to the conference room and sat down and looked at her expectantly. "Here's the basic test we'll give each student to determine their literacy levels. Some of our students may not speak English, some may. We will probably have native speakers of English mixed with immigrant students, so we need to be prepared for everyone.

"One important thing to remember is that some of our students who are immigrants may not speak English but are educated already from schooling in their home countries. For those students, it's easy to move them through the program quickly because they're already literate. The students who have little or no education in their home countries will take much longer to acquire literacy.

"The other students we may encounter are Texas high school dropouts. Some of these students quit school because of family responsibilities and were helping their parents support the family at a young age. They are usually fluent English speakers even if they're native Spanish speakers. Others likely have learning disabilities and were never diagnosed to be given special education services. Others missed too much school and got so far behind that they could never catch up. We will have some former gang members probably whose education was interrupted by incarceration. So, be prepared for any and all."

"Gang members? Incarcerated?" Courtney asked with a tremor in her voice.

"Yes, maybe. Maybe not. My point in telling you is that I don't want you to be surprised Monday morning. Adult education students are not the kids you went to high school and hung out with. Whatever their stories, it's none of our business unless they volunteer personal information. Also, some may be undocumented, but never ask about their legal citizenship status. Again, it's none of our business. If the college cares, they will ask those questions. I'll give you a list of personal questions that you may ask them, but don't pry. Students who end up here are often discouraged about their ability to learn but feel the need to learn more to get their GED's if possible. At the very least, the non-English speakers want to learn enough English to navigate their lives here."

"I've told you a lot of the more problematic features of our prospective students, so let me finish by saying I spent two consecutive calendar years teaching adults rather than shorter public school calendar years and found them to be the most motivated, hard-working students I'd ever seen. Adults understand the need for education to help them in their jobs, to get a job, to make more money, or to be a role model for their kids. That's the neat part of adult education. You do not have to deal with a bunch of spoiled kids who are just coming to school to socialize. That's what public school is like. The older they get in K-12 public schools, the more the students can try your patience. I've coached new teachers and know their frustrations because I had the same frustrations when I first started teaching years ago. I will coach you both so you will be successful in this job. So, don't worry. If you have a problem, all you have to do is bring it to me and I'll help you figure it out.

"More questions?"

"No. I guess not. Can we have a few minutes to look over this basic test?" Trace asked as he glanced at the test Ellie had given him wondering just how he was going to make it through this job. He couldn't wait till lunch when he and Courtney could really talk without Ellie's hearing what they had to say.

'Well, I can see I've scared them shitless. What spineless wimps. Oh hell, I'd probably be afraid of teaching adults too if I were their age. What am I saying? No, I wouldn't. I'd be thrilled to be challenged, but that trait seems to have escaped this generation. Now I'm babbling to myself. Crap!'

The day passed quickly, and Ellie was relieved to see that Trace and Courtney returned from lunch and on time. After the looks on their faces this morning, she was afraid they'd just run for it and ditch their jobs.

"I just got the rosters in my e-mail inbox so let me print them out and we'll go over the student lists and see who we've got. Does that sound good?" Ellie said and looked at her team expectantly.

"Sure. Great," Trace said and tried to smile. Courtney just nodded her head. Here we go, Ellie said as she pulled the sheets of paper from the printer. Let's sit down together and look at these and make a game plan. I'll make copies of the students that you'll be mainly in charge of. Until we determine skill levels, this will just be a starting point that we'll adjust as we see what our students' needs are. Oh, I forgot to mention this morning when you looked so freaked out. You don't have to say anything, I noticed," Ellie said as she saw the looks on their faces.

"If there are any difficult students, I'll handle them. You don't have to worry about any student being too much for you to handle. Any problem students will be my territory. I don't expect any because as I said before, most students who end up in adult education classes are positively motivated and are really no trouble. As you know I was an administrator for the last eight years of my public school career and I'm used to handling problems of any kind, especially unruly students. Now, relax and let's look at these students."

Ellie noticed that there were all white students on the rosters and knowing the demographics for the area, wondered where the Black and Hispanic students were and made a mental note to go recruiting.

"Just by looking at the names, it doesn't look like we have any ESL students to start with so we'll assume that basic literacy and GED prep will be the initial focus till I can go out into the communities and recruit a little for our program. Now, which one of you wants to work with students who need to learn to read and write?"

Courtney raised her hand and Ellie said, "Excellent, Courtney. The key to success with basic literacy is to take care not to embarrass the students who are already sensitive about the fact that they're illiterate. It'll be important to structure what you teach them in a way to build confidence and build success into each day. Be compassionate with them and don't let them become discouraged. Does that make sense?"

"Yes, I think I can do that. It can't be too hard, right?" Courtney said in her quiet voice.

"No, it's not too hard and I'll help you with anything you need. I've taught basic students and it's wonderful when you see them smile after learning to write their names. Did you know that most of them sign their names with an 'X'? Learning to sign their names is tedious but gives them so much pride."

"Uh, what do you want me to teach, Miss Ellie?" Trace asked, for once looking sincere.

"Well, I think GED prep would be a great fit because of emphasis on reading and writing in the English portion of the test. Also, you can teach the social studies part that maybe Courtney can split with you since she has some history in her background. Do either of you feel like you could teach the math portion? It's basically elementary math up through algebra with a little geometry thrown in."

"Not math!" Trace and Courtney both said with concerned looks on their faces.

"What is it with math? Everyone says that. Not to worry, you two. I'll take the math classes as well as any ESL students that we have. That sounds like a plan. Now, let's divide this up for testing, which will be the first thing we do on Monday once we determine we've got the right people in our class. The first day of classes on any campus always seems to find students in the wrong class at some point. That should only take a few minutes. Can one of you make 3 copies of these rosters, so we have a master list plus one for each of us. OK?"

Trace actually volunteered to go back to the office to make copies, and Ellie was pleased and hopeful that he was changing his previously shitty attitude for the better. Courtney still looked shell-shocked though and Ellie was worried about her and hoped she would stick with her new job.

"Thanks, Trace. Now, let's just leave all these things here and both of you need to head over to administration to get your parking stickers. Be sure to find the faculty window or you'll be there all day. I used the online registration this morning and it still took a half hour. I know it's nowhere near 5:00 yet, but once you get your stickers, just go home for the weekend and I'll see you Monday morning at 8 a.m. Alright?"

"Thanks, Ellie,' Courtney said quietly, and Trace looked surprised and happy as he got up to join Courtney who was making a beeline for the door.

Ellie sighed and closed the conference room and went looking for the morning's head custodian before the other head man got in for the evening shift that came on at three. As she understood it, the morning and evening shifts overlapped an hour, so he should be there either way. She wandered around till she found him in his office in the next building.

"Hi, Mr. Jenkins. We met briefly a few days ago. I'm Ellie Thompson, the new adult ed director/ teacher and I'd like to ask you for a favor. Do you have a minute right now?"

Getting up, Davis Jenkins said, "I hope you're not here to tell me they haven't cleaned your rooms right already."

Putting out her hand to shake hands, Ellie grasped Mr. Jenkins' hand and laughed. "No, that's not it. My rooms look great. No complaints. What I want to talk to you about is a bit more delicate."

"Now you've made me curious. OK. Let's have it, Ms. Thompson," Davis sat as he sat back down and motioned for Ellie to take a seat.

"Please, Mr. Jenkins, just Ellie. What I want is some advice about where I could recruit some African American students who might be interested in our adult education program here. When I looked at the rosters today, all the students signed up are white. That's fine, but since I know that there's diversity in our community, I'd like to see if anyone in the African American community would be willing to give us a try. Oh, I'll also be trying to recruit in the Hispanic community too should the question come up. If there have never been any dropouts from either of those communities, I'll be thrilled. However, statistics show that dropouts usually come from all segments of a community's population."

"Well, that's a surprise having you come here. Why'd you choose me? Maybe I don't know any Black folk around here," Davis Jenkins said while watching Ellie's face for her reaction.

"Well, I chose you because I've only met three people here: Mr. Morris, Mr. Vasquez and you. That's why I started with you and if you truly don't know any African American people around town, then I hope you'll give me an idea of where to start meeting some people who could help me," Ellie said with a wry expression.

"Well, what are the odds of that? White, Hispanic and Black. You've met one of each of us then. I'm surprised you want to find more students, but I'll stop giving you a hard time and help you out because I'm glad you want to teach people who may not know much about this program. The past few years the teachers weren't very motivated, so a lot of people gave up on the program when they figured out they just weren't learning much, and nobody ever passed the GED exam. That made the classes just a waste of time as far as people could see and they didn't have time to waste like that or money to throw away on the tests. I do know some people and I'll put the word out to round up a few more students here for you. I wish I could say that every Black student graduated, but sadly they didn't, and I think this program could help our entire town. I'm gonna take a chance on you and help you out if I can. Thank you, Miss Ellie," Davis said as he shook her hand again.

Ellie smiled happily and thanked Mr. Jenkins for his help and turned to go when he said, "Aren't you the one that asked one of my custodians to eat lunch at the table with the college human resources manager? Pretty bold of you."

"Yes, it was me and it didn't seem bold to me though I'm learning that other people here might see that differently. Are you one of those people, Mr. Jenkins?"

"Miss Ellie, I don't care who you eat lunch with or what color they are, but not everyone around here feels that way so don't be surprised if some people don't take kindly to the kind of mixing you're proposing. Some people get pretty upset about it and that's a fact."

"Thank you for the advice, Mr. Jenkins, but I suspect I'm too old to change my ways on things like that. Consider me advised and warned. I appreciate your taking the time to tell me. No one around here seems to like to say what they're thinking. I guess I spent too many years up north where people say what they think. No sugar coating like down here. I guess it goes along with that awful sweet tea that they serve everywhere."

"Oh, no. Don't badmouth our sweet tea or you'll never make friends here. It's a well-loved tradition; And you'd better start calling me David. I don't respond well to Mr. Jenkins," Davis Jenkins said with a laugh.

"Duly noted and warned. Thank you. See you Monday," Ellie said, gave Mr. Jenkins a wave, turned and left his office.

"Interesting. I'm beginning to wonder what I was thinking about coming back to rural, small-town Texas. So many traditions and not all of them are so innocuous. They opposed racial mixing as they called it back when I first came to Texas decades ago. Still stuck in the past. Too late."

After a dinner that Flo had warming in the oven, ready for Ellie's return, they lingered at the table a while and got refills for their unsweet tea. "Well, I think you have something else to tell me about your day. Now spill it," Flo ordered with a sly smile.

"You always did have that kind of creepy psychic ability or whatever you call it to know when to ask the right question, Auntie Flo. You're right. There is something else. Noé came to my office to walk me to my car again and he also asked me for a date tomorrow night," Ellie said and waited for Flo's response, knowing she'd be thrilled for her.

"Yes! I knew there was something to his flirting with you even though you said he wasn't. He's interested in you, or he wouldn't have asked you out. I get to meet him! I get to meet him! You understand that if I don't like him, all of this may have to radically change, yes?"

"Flo, settle down and are you planning on shoving him out the door tomorrow night if you don't approve? I won't let you do that, so wipe that thought out of your mind. You're going to have to promise to behave or I won't have him come to the house to pick me up and you won't be meeting him. How does that sound?"

"Cruel and unusual. You know I wouldn't embarrass you unless I think he looks like prison material. I mean, how picky are they in hiring custodians? Stop. I know you're going to say that I'm not giving you credit to be able to be a good judge of character. Right?"

"Well, it seems like you've just had this whole conversation with yourself and concluded that it might just be alright. So, relax till tomorrow night when he comes here. I have to admit that I'm looking forward to going out with him. I haven't been on a date since Chad, and I am out of practice."

"You wasted five years of your life with that loser you married, stayed around to raise those kids of his and then ran to upstate NY to hide out."

"Well, Auntie Flo. Don't hold back. I know you never really liked Chad though his family didn't seem to have much trouble worming their way into your affection."

"I did love those kids of his. Funny thing is that they preferred you to him when you decided to divorce him. Don't they still keep in touch with you?"

"Yes. That was the best part of that marriage. I do love those kids of his. I never dared hope they'd still keep me in their lives, but they did," Ellie said with a sigh.

"Kept you in their lives? That's an understatement. Even though the court said they had to go with their biological father, they spent most of their time at your house.

That's what's funny. You were a good mother to those kids, and it never mattered to them that you didn't birth them."

"I wish I had; then I wouldn't even have to deal with Chad ever again. That lying, cheating, son of a bitch still pisses me off whenever I see him because I have to question my sanity for ever marrying him," Ellie said with annoyance.

"That's done and you can't go back, but you just need to remember that you wouldn't have those four kids in your life if you hadn't married that loser. That's your gold at the end of that rainbow,"

"I know. I know. Fortunately, they're all adults now and I don't have to see Chad very often as a result. Geez. I was a stupid fool. But enough of my sordid past. Let's go out to eat tonight to celebrate that I'm going to have a steady paycheck coming in. How's that sound?

Chapter 3: The Date

Noé arrived at Ellie's house promptly at 6:30 and knocked on the door and was surprised when an older woman opened the door slightly out of breath.

"Er, good evening. Is Ellie there?" Noé said with a smile, figuring he'd learn about her roommate soon.

Ellie's head peeked out behind her aunts and said, "Hi, Noé. Come on in and meet my Aunt Flo who can run faster than I can apparently. Yes, we raced to the door, if you're wondering though I'm feeling like an adolescent to admit that just now," Ellie said with a blush.

"Hello, Aunt Flo. It's nice to meet you," Noé said and grasped the hand that Flo extended toward him. "You did say 'raced,' didn't you? Should I ask why or just ignore that comment?"

"Ignore it!" Ellie said as she grabbed her jacket and purse off the hall table and then gave her aunt a hug. "Night, Auntie Flo. Behave yourself while I'm gone."

Laughing, Flo closed the door behind them as she watched Noé walk down the sidewalk with her niece. *'Nice looking man. I do see what Ellie meant about his accent. Sounds very foreign. Looks like he's just the right age for her and he is definitely taller than she is; I know she doesn't like to date short men.'*

"I didn't know you had a roommate, Ellie. Your Aunt Flo is a bit of a character, I think," Noé commented once they were in his truck.

"That's an understatement, Noé. She lives in Trinidad, Colorado, but turned up a

few days ago to surprise me saying she came
down to babysit my dog Duke who is
currently hanging out in the backyard or
you'd have met him too. She's my
godmother and was my favorite aunt when I
was growing up and is not as old as my
other aunts and uncles. Though she was
older, she always felt like more of a
contemporary. I always could and still do
talk to her about anything. That hasn't
changed from the time we spent together
growing up. She's got a big heart," Ellie
explained.

"I can see that she cares about you. It
must be nice to have some family here in a
new town for you," Noé said wistfully.

"Well, I guess that's my opening to ask
you about your family. Do you have family
in town? Do you have any roommates? I
hope you won't tell me you have a female
one, but I forgot to ask that before I said
'yes' to going out with you tonight."

Laughing, Noe said, "No family in town
and no roommates of the human kind though
I do have a dog also. Her name is Lola. She
keeps me company and is an excellent
listener, though I do wish sometimes that my
roommate could talk back to me."

"I know just how you feel. Duke has
always been my best sounding board, and he

has kept me from being lonely more times than I can count, but there is something about human conversation that I miss at times, too," Ellie said with a sigh.

"I'm glad we're going out tonight, Ellie Thompson. I think we're going to be friends and I'm looking forward to spending this evening with you. Now, let me ask if you've ever been to a *charreada* which is a Mexican style rodeo?"

"No, I haven't though I've seen photos of people riding in them. Is that where we're going? I'd really like to see one," Ellie said enthusiastically.

"Yes, it is where we're going, and the photos don't do the riders justice. It's quite a show. I think you're going to enjoy tonight and I'm glad you're looking forward to going. I must admit I wasn't sure how you'd react but hoped for the best. There will also be music in between some of the events."

"I'm really excited about tonight's rodeo you're taking us to, Noé. It should be a lot of fun. I love horses and I love all things Mexican."

Turning to look at her with a smile, Noé reached over and pulled her closer. "You do remember that I'm Mexican, right? Does that statement you just made include me?"

Ellie's face turned red, and she could feel the blush traveling down her neck to her chest. "Well, I guess we'll have to see about that, Mr. Vasquéz," Ellie said smiling while she kept her face down and looked away out the window again though she did stay seated closer to Noé on the seat.

They turned at a sign that said, "Rancho Dos Ríos" and went down a gravel lane under the horizontal cross piece that suspended a metal sign with the ranch's name on it. There were signs hanging on the fence saying *"Esta noche/Tonight."* The lane seemed to go on forever to Ellie who bounced on the seat a few times as the truck rolled over some potholes in the farm road that went on and on. There was barbed wire fence on both sides of the gravel road and the delicate leaves of mesquite and huisache trees framing the road like sentinels standing watch at random were visible against the darkening sky, bright with oranges and reds. The sun was going down; it was just starting to get dark, and they could see spotlights in the distance.

As they drew closer, there were cars lining the arena area, surrounding it. Ellie saw horse trailers and pickups everywhere with people walking around quickly getting ready and hurrying around in colorful costumes. Men were coming out of trailers and putting on big hats, *sombreros,* and pulling down shirt sleeves, showing the white cuffs. Ellie noticed the elaborately designed and decorated outfits on the men and saw a few women starting to come out of other trailers wearing long, flowing dresses with ruffled skirts.

"Oh, look, there are women, too!"

"Yes, they are *escaramuzas* (cowgirls that are choreographed female horse riders) wearing *Adelita* dresses. History and legend say that during the revolution, the escaramuzas would ride out together raising a lot of dust to trick the *federales,* who were the government soldiers, so they would be misled and not follow the revolutionaries. I suspect history would also verify they did that, but in some towns, they were almost mythical in how people spoke of these brave women. I doubt the *federales* were happy when they caught up with the women and discovered that they had been tricked. Today, they continue the tradition and still ride the old-style saddle, the *albarda,* but I'm not sure what you call that in English. My English is not so good all the time.

"You've got to be kidding me. Your English is fabulous, but I think the word you're looking for must be 'sidesaddle' if those saddles on that group of horses over there is what you're talking about. Not a common piece of riding equipment today to be sure," Ellie said and pointed at the horses over by the fence that the women were approaching. Unless they study the history of horseback riding, most people wouldn't know that word in any language or culture.

"Yes, sidesaddle is the right word, and you don't need to flatter me about my English as I know I'm hard to understand. I get those looks from people every day at work when I talk to them," Noé said with a wry look on his face.

"I'm probably once again overstepping my boundaries, but do you want to know why people have trouble understanding you sometimes?" Ellie asked and held her breath, hoping that she hadn't angered Noé. *'But he did bring it up. It's not like I offered this analysis out of the blue.'*

Noé just looked at Ellie for a minute and then with a resigned look said, "I get the feeling that you're about to start bouncing up and down if I don't let you tell me. So, tell me."

"You are incredibly fluent with an amazing vocabulary, but it's your intonation, the rhythm of your speech that throws them off. It's something I could help

you with if you'd like some day. I have a
master's in bilingual and ESL and this is
what I do, but only if you'd want to. You're
clearly an educated man and I think it must
be frustrating to have people look at you
with that mystified look they give you when
they don't understand you," Ellie finished in
a rush and looked over at Noé for his
reaction, hoping she hadn't pissed him off.
She didn't want him to turn around at this
point and take her home because he was
furious about her meddling and put off by
the direction their date had suddenly taken.

Surprisingly, Noé smiled and said,
"Private tutoring? Just you and me? What
man wouldn't want to sign up for that class?
It sounds like a good idea. Tell me when we
start. My only condition is that I don't want
you to turn into my teacher when we're out
on a date. Deal?"

"Deal," Ellie said and relaxed. She felt
relieved that she hadn't offended Noé and
glad that it seemed that their date would
continue, and he wouldn't just literally
throw up his hands and take her back home.

They continued their walk through the
staging area and made their way up to the
bleachers which were made of wood and
looked like they'd been there for years. Paint
was peeling off the wooden boards leaving a

weathered grey exposed. The steps up had a groove hollowed out in the middle of each where many, many people had stepped through the years on their way up to the bench seats. Surprisingly, the steps felt strong and sturdy and none the worst for wear given their apparent age. They found seats near the center about midway up and settled in to watch the first event start as some men rode into the arena, urging their horses forward at breathtaking speeds.

Ellie watched, mesmerized, enjoying the beauty of the horses, their coats shiny, their nostrils spread wide open with the effort they expended to gallop around the arena. Almost before she knew what was happening, Ellie saw one of the men jump from his horse onto the back of another horse as it drew up beside it. Unbelievably, the cowboy was able to stay upright on the new horse and continue the frenzy around the arena.

"Wow! That was amazing!" Ellie gushed and looked over at Noé and found him watching her, his eyes showing some emotion that she was unsure of. "What? Did you see that?"

Noé smiled and nodded, "Many times. When I was young, I even rode in some *charreadas*. It's exhilarating and probably dangerous, but when you're young, danger isn't something you always acknowledge."

"Probably dangerous? That's surely an understatement. Oh, look, Noé, here come the women!" Ellie said and looked back to the arena. The women rode their horses around the arena in formation and executed both simple and complicated drills. The pageantry was enthralling.

"I wish I'd brought my camera. This is incredible. Oh, Noé, thank you for bringing me here. I've never seen Mexican cowboys and cowgirls ride like this. I've probably seen some of the costumes in parades here and there. After all, we are in Texas, which used to be part of Mexico, so Mexican heritage is celebrated here. And everyone celebrates Cinco de Mayo, even in upstate New York," Ellie said laughingly.

"Don't get me started on Cinco de Mayo. It's hard to believe how people have made that such a big deal when it's not so in Mexico. I guess restaurants and bars needed a May holiday where people would drink and party, something they'd hardly do for Mother's Day."

"You're probably right. That's funny though," Ellie agreed. "Oh, Noé, look over there. Do you see the mariachi group? Listen. They're starting to play. Ellie noticed that Noé sang along with the mariachis as they played and sang several songs during an intermission.

After the sun set, Noé and Ellie got up to leave and were making their way towards the stairs when one of the *escaramuzas* came along the front walkway and went up and jumped at Noé, wrapped her arms around him and tried to reach up and kiss him.

Looking uncomfortable, Noé unwrapped her arms and gently pushed her away. "Hello, Carmen."

"¿Eso es todo? No me has llamado por muchos meses y ahora que te veo, ¿no me das nada, ni un besito? Y por qué estás con esta bolilla?" (That's it? You haven't called me for many months and now that I do see you, you don't give me anything, not even a little kiss? And why are you with this white woman/honky?"

"Ellie, I'd like to introduce you to Carmen, but we have to be leaving," Noé said and grasped Ellie's hand to hurry her along and away from the situation.

"Nice meeting you," Ellie said looking back at Carmen who was looking murderously at her.

They walked down the steps with Carmen still cursing at them. Both heard the

word *puta* (whore) several times but just
kept walking at Noé's urging. As they
turned to go to the truck, Noé took hold of
Ellie's hand again and then pulled her close
next to him. When she was at his side, he
wrapped his arm around her waist, keeping
her close as they walked on.

"Sorry you had to meet her and that she
caused a scene. She hasn't been coming to
these for quite a while and honestly, I didn't
even think that she might be here."

"I guess it's none of my business, but it
seems like she feels like you're betraying
her being here with me. Just what is she to
you, if you don't mind my asking?" Ellie
said, looking up and seeing Noé's jaw
clench, exasperation clearly on his face.

"It would have been none of your
business if she hadn't created a scandal like
she usually does. I might have said 'hi'' but
that's it. She and I dated a few times last
year and she was upset when I told her I
didn't want to date any more. Upset
probably doesn't cover it, though. She was
furious and seemed to think that we had a
relationship that was something more
involved. We only dated a few times, and I
only kissed her once.

"Too much information, I know, but I
want you to be sure that I don't have a

girlfriend lurking around every corner waiting to ambush us. The Mexican community around here tends to gossip, and everybody knows everyone else's business because we're small in numbers. It was about this time last year when we went out. I don't know what fantasy she's created in her mind about our non-relationship, but she's gone over the edge as far as I'm concerned."

"You must be some kisser if she's still thinking about that one kiss," Ellie said in a teasing tone.

Noé laughed and said, "I can't wait to show you, Ellie. I hope you think so."

When they were back in the truck, Noé navigated the deeply rutted farm road slowly till they finally reached the paved highway. Turning right, he headed toward El Campo, a slightly larger town than Wharton where they both lived and worked. Thankfully, it was freeway, so the road was smooth, and they quickly arrived at the edge of town.

"I hope you're hungry enough for a little snack. I have a favorite little place I'd like to show you." Noé said as he pulled up in front of a small restaurant that was brightly lit and had brightly painted walls to match.

"I've never seen this place, and I've been in this area a few times since I moved here. What is it?"

"It's called Petra's and it's small but has the best home-cooked meals. She makes her tortillas fresh all day long, but is only open Friday, Saturday and Sunday. She says she has enough to do with raising her six sons without working in a restaurant every day. Most of them work here helping her, but I think it's more to keep an eye on them as they're all teenagers. I think she's smart."

They went inside and it was small, with only six tables. Someone was just finishing so one of Petra's sons took them to that table where another son was cleaning off the dishes and wiping the plastic tablecloth. Noé held Ellie's chair for her and then took his own seat.

"What? Why are you looking at me like that?" Noé asked when he noticed Ellie's expression.

"Noé, I can't remember when a man held out a chair for me and waited to seat me before sitting down. That was nice, very nice."

"What kind of men have you been going out with, Ellie? They must not be gentlemen."

"Don't be scared, but I haven't been on a date since I got divorced."

"How long ago was your divorce, Ellie?" Noé asked, curious because Ellie really

85

hadn't shared much information about her life before she came to Wharton.

"Ten years ago." Ellie said with a small voice. "I know that may sound like a long time, but I've been busy," she said defensively.

"Ten years! Ellie, that's a really long time not to date. Maybe you'll tell me about it sometime."

"Maybe. My life before here had a few bumps in the road, but I'm here starting over now and want to focus on present-time now and what's ahead in the future. Does that make sense?" Ellie asked, hoping Noé wouldn't press her for details just yet. She liked him a lot and felt very comfortable with him but wasn't ready to go into details of her life before being back here.

"What do you recommend? I am hungry. I guess watching all those riders made me feel like I was exercising along with them."

After dinner, Noé walked Ellie around to her side of the truck and after he opened her door. He reached to grab her waist to help her up but decided it was time to see if a kiss would work for Ellie right now. He'd been waiting all evening for just this chance. He leaned down a little and softly cupped her face with his hand and slowly moved his lips over hers, tasting her gently. Ellie surprised him and herself when she reached up to put her hands behind his head to pull him into the kiss. Before they knew it, they were both kissing each other eagerly, and Ellie opened for Noé when his tongue touched her lips. Then they were kissing deeply and instinctively moved their bodies closer. Noé pulled Ellie's body into his and he knew she could feel his erection as their bodies closely met.

Breathing hard, Noé said, "Ellie, Ellie, *por Dios* (oh my God), what the hell is happening to me? You taste so good. I don't want to stop kissing you. I feel like I've been waiting a very long time to kiss someone like you."

"Noé, I can't get enough of you either. I can see why that woman wanted another kiss from you. If we don't stop this now, we're going to be ripping our clothes off right here in the parking lot, which I'm actually considering right now in case you wondered."

Noé laughed as he tucked a strand of Ellie's hair back behind her ear. "You're right, *mi amor*, (my love) Let's get into the truck while we still can."

They got on the road, heading out of El Campo back to Wharton and were quiet for a while, both thinking about their kiss. They had both been taken by surprise by the depth of feeling the kiss had evoked. Neither had thought that their date tonight would get so serious when both had been looking for a light-hearted evening, not a moment that felt like it had changed their relationship irrevocably.

"Ellie, I don't want to offend you, but if you'd like to do a little more of that kissing like we just did, I know a place we can go that won't involve offending your aunt or passersby. Tell me what you want me to do."

"Noé, I actually am at a loss for words, which you know never happens to me. I think you'd just better take me home. We can shake hands on the porch to play it safe."

"Whatever you want. A handshake is probably a good idea."

"No, wait, Noé. I do want you to kiss me some more, but you scare me."

"Scare you? What?!" Noé said, angry and a little hurt.

"No, silly, Not that way. I feel very safe with you. You scare me because that kiss scared me. I still don't know what to think about the way you made me feel. That's what scares me. I thought we'd have fun tonight, which we did and maybe make plans to go out again. I like you Noé, but I didn't expect to have those feelings when you kissed me. I don't know when a man has kissed me like you did," Ellie said and looked over at Noé, hoping she'd clarified her thoughts enough that he wasn't still offended by what she'd said. She'd heard the anger in his voice and the hurt a moment ago and he was such a good man, that she didn't want to hurt his feelings in any way.

"When you put it that way, I get what you mean. I don't know what to think either about that kiss. If we'd have been anywhere else, I'd have taken your clothes off and mine too to see what else we could discover together. I liked how you made me feel and it's been a while for me too, Ellie. Maybe we're both out of practice and that's why it felt like it did."

Laughing, Ellie said, "Noé that didn't feel out of practice to me. It was wonderful and made me think of things I haven't considered for many years."

"Alright, Ellie, I'm going to take you home now before we decide to take this further than either one of us planned tonight though it is tempting now. We don't have to be in a hurry or rush anything. I do want to see you again, Ellie. I hope you want to see me again too."

"Cripes. I'm having flashbacks to high school all of a sudden though I didn't have conversations like this one then. You make me feel like a girl again, Noé. I'm afraid we're in danger of thinking this to death though. Too much talking can ruin a moment."

"OK. Now you've got my head spinning. Does that mean you don't want to go home just yet? Am I allowed to say how hopeful that makes me feel without scaring you again?"

"Yes. I mean. No, I don't want you to take me home right now after all. This may not be a good idea, but I want to spend some more time with you if you're willing," Ellie explained and looked over at Noé's smile spreading as she'd continued talking. Gone was the frown from before and in its place was a pleased look on his face.

"I suggest we go to my place rather than yours. You have your aunt staying there and I don't know if I'm ready to confront her again. I have to be more on my game before I take her on again. Plus, I'd like us to have privacy rather than being under your aunt's microscope."

Laughing, Ellie agreed, "Yes, let's go to your place. I agree that my Auntie Flo is waiting there to pounce on me and grill me

for details. You also would have to get
slobbered on by my dog Duke. Your place
sounds much simpler."

Soon, they turned into a neighborhood
that had tall, towering trees that were visible
even in the darkening light, silhouetted
against the sky. The road was narrow and
winding. They drove all the way back into
the neighborhood and arrived at what looked
like the last house on the lane. Ellie
struggled to see the house and yard, but it
was too dark and there was no yard light.
Noé got out of his truck and came around to
open Ellie's door. He took her hand and
helped her step down and then turned to go
up the walk that had motion-activated lights
that lit as they approached, still holding her
hand in his.

When they got to the front door, Ellie
said, "I wish I could see what your house
looks like Noé. I like how it's all the way
down this lane. No neighbors are next door
and there can't be much traffic down this
road as it's narrow and winding. That should
discourage speeders at any rate."

"It is private and secluded and not that far
from town. We're out in the county here
rather than inside the city limits, but I
bought this place without having even
visited it. I was still in Mexico but knew

where I wanted to end up here in the States. I had friends who used to pass through this area when they were coming home from Ohio where they picked tomatoes."

"Whoa, that sounds like migrant farm work and yes, Wharton would be on that route back to the Rio Grande Valley. You certainly don't seem like that would be your crowd though. How'd that happen?"

"Actually, I'd met them in Mexico when they were there studying, and we kept up the friendship through the years. More questions later. We're standing outside when we could be inside and much more comfortable. Let's go."

Ellie agreed and followed Noé inside into a large entryway and continued after him into the living room. He went over to the fireplace and turned on the gas and the gas logs lit with the flames moving in a line along the top of the logs and providing a warm glow to the room. Noé returned to where Ellie was standing and took her coat and draped it along with his over the chair near them and took her hand to lead her to the sofa facing the fireplace.

They sat down on the oversized sofa and as she sank down onto the soft cushions, ran her hand over the butter soft leather and wondered how the hell a custodian could afford furniture like this along with this house that had a least one huge room in it and had looked quite large in the dark outside when they had approached it. It just didn't fit. He didn't fit with his heavy accented but rich English vocabulary and his almost courtly manners. At least he didn't fit her stereotype of custodian as she mentally chastised herself for having said stereotype to begin with. *'I thought I was beyond judging people like that. It's just that he's got me thrown off track somehow. Crap, I hope he's not some drug cartel guy on the run here in the States. That would explain all these expensive things, this house, his clothes, his job to hide who he truly was. Stop! You're letting your imagination write a whole novel here about him without giving him a chance to explain just what's going on.'*

Breaking into her thoughts, Noé said, "Ellie, could I get you some wine, or would you prefer coffee or a soda?"

"I'd love some coffee if it's not too much trouble, Noé."

Noé smiled, got up and turned to leave the living room and Ellie followed, trailing along and was surprised to see how far he walked till he got to the huge kitchen that looked like it was equipped with state-of-the-art appliances. They passed through an area with some bookshelves on either side and Ellie saw framed diplomas and certificates with Noé's name on them. Wanting to stop to read them without making a big deal, Ellie promised herself she'd look at them in detail later. Maybe they contained the answers to all her questions about this house and Noé's educated speech and manners.

The kitchen also didn't disappoint in surprises with its all-stainless-steel appliances, granite countertops that had a beautiful, strong pattern and beautiful high-end wood cabinets. The backsplash was glass subway tile and completed the look. His industrial size gas stove had a pot filler over it with a custom hood, and the sink was a massive farmhouse sink with an apron front, and an industrial-looking pull down faucet and sprayer.

"Wow! This is some kitchen, Noé! Don't tell me you're a gourmet cook also," Ellie said and looked at him questioningly. The more she saw of this house, the more worried she became about how his custodian's salary afforded this caliber home. Hopefully the answers were in those framed certificates she was dying to see.

"No, I wish I could say that I was, but this kitchen was here when I bought this house and occasionally, I do hire a caterer to come in to cook when I throw a big party. I don't do that often though, so usually, it just sits here and gets a once-a-week cleaning by a local cleaning service. I spend my days picking up after other people and cleaning so I'm not eager to do more of it when I get home from work," Noé said wryly and smiled.

That smile of his is killer and totally makes me forget whatever the hell I was trying to focus on. I'm lost here.'

Noe went over to his own coffee maker that looked like the high-class version of Ellie's Keurig that she kept in her office and pulled out a tray of various coffee blends in their little cups. "What's your pleasure?"

"Um, I'd like some decaf if you have it, Noé. That would be great. Thanks."

Noé clearly knew his way around his coffee machine and in moments, was putting a hand thrown mug in front of Ellie who'd chosen a spot on one of the bar stools to sit and watch him. Reflexively, Ellie grabbed the mug and wrapped her fingers around it and inhaled the aroma.

"For decaf, this smells delicious. And this mug is beautiful. Don't tell me you're a potter in your spare time and mix your own glazes to get results like this."

"Well, I won't tell you then," Noé said and laughed as Ellie's jaw dropped in surprise.

"I was kidding!" Ellie exclaimed.

"I'm not. I learned how to throw pots on a wheel about fifteen years ago along with my daughter to give her something to do when she was recuperating."

"Oh, Noé, is this the part of the conversation when you remember to tell me that you're married, and your wife doesn't understand you?" Ellie said and got down off the stool, ready to leave.

"Ah, no, Ellie. I'm not married, but I was, and yes, she didn't understand me, and I didn't understand her. I think I loved her daughter more than her in the end. She's my stepdaughter technically, but I love her like she was my own flesh and blood. Her name's Graciela."

"Sorry, Noé for jumping to bad conclusions. I shouldn't have reacted like that, but I did have a moment there when I was pissed to think that you could have kissed me and brought me here when you had a wife hiding somewhere. Really pissed actually. My ex cheated on me a lot and that's just a sore subject for me."

"Ellie, I wouldn't do that and especially not to you. I kissed you because I like you and I thought you liked me at least a little too. There are no women hiding out somewhere that I should be telling you about. I planned on telling you about Graciela later tonight. I thought we could sit and get to know each other better. Am I right on that still? Or do you want me to take you home because you are still pissed as you put it?"

"No. I'm good. I'd like to talk and get to know you better. All our conversations seem to end too soon because we're places where we can't really be alone and talk in depth about anything. I have things I guess I should tell you too. Fair's fair, after all," Ellie said and looked at Noé and smiled as he reached across the counter to cover her hand with his.

Ellie watched as Noé turned her hand palm up and ran his fingers over her palm and eventually laced his fingers with hers. Ellie felt lust stirring in her belly as his fingers stroked her palm, the calluses rough against her hand. It gave her internal shivers as he continued to explore her hand in such intimate detail. It was a relief when he laced his fingers through hers because she was starting to feel ridiculous by her reaction.

'Shit. I'm getting turned on and the man is just running his fingers over my hand. I must just be horny. It's been too long since I got laid as Aunt Flo would say.'

Noé came around the counter, still holding Ellie's hand in his and came up to stand in front of her. He put his arm around her waist and pulled her body into his and Ellie could feel his erection pushing against her belly and was glad to see that she wasn't the only one turned on with just minimal contact and felt a little better.

"Come, *mi amor* (my love). Let's go sit in front of the fire to drink our coffee. It's nice in there and we can talk and tell each other our secrets."

They walked back down the wide-open hallway till they got back to the living room. The fire did make the room look warm and welcoming. Noé moved the coffee table closer so they could set their cups on it and then leaned back into the comfy sofa. He put his arm around Ellie's shoulder and snuggled her up against him and said, "Well, who starts? Do you want to tell me what you meant by some things you probably should tell me?"

"Sure. It's old history now, but I was married before too. My ex-husband Chad cheated on me multiple times and when I couldn't tolerate even seeing him anymore, I divorced him. I stayed with him much too long because I didn't want to lose the kids which he had legal right to as their biological parent. The funny thing is that while Chad brought the four kids to our marriage and he did get custody as he's their biological father, they continued to live with me. They told him he'd screwed up the marriage, and they weren't letting his stupidity break up their happy home. I think he didn't know what to say and just let them live with me though they did visit him occasionally till he got married again. They were pretty much just disgusted with him and so was I. So, I have four kids, sort of, but they're grown now and on their own. They do stop in to visit me from time to time though. And that's all of my secrets."

"Really? That wasn't too bad."

"Oh, wait. I forgot. I had cancer a few years back, but I'm OK now. That's thankfully behind me."

"*Dios mío* (my God), Ellie. That's a lot in one breath. Let me tell you more about Graciela and myself because I haven't been completely honest with you. Now wait, Ellie. I can see that you on your face and feel how tense you just got. No wife. Remember. No wife."

Ellie looked at Noé and didn't see anything to alarm her in his face, only honesty and caring. She figured it couldn't be that bad or he wouldn't look so relaxed. It did make her stomach tie itself in knots with worry. This relationship had barely gotten off the ground and was already getting much too complicated. Deciding to think positively, Ellie gave Noé a small smile and nodded to him.

"When I married Graciela's mother Valeria, I was much younger and has just started my career as a civil engineer. I had graduated early, so was only just twenty, ready for my twenty-first birthday in a few months. She was thirty, ten years older and much more experienced in the ways of the world and love. She dazzled me with her glamour and money. It was a crazy thing how we met and became a couple within weeks. Valeria and I got married soon after. I loved her daughter from the first time I saw her. I wanted more children, but Valeria is an artist, a dancer, and didn't want another pregnancy to interfere with her career. That was how our arguing started. I wanted to make a home for Graciela, but Valeria's career took her away from us often.

Graciela was injured in a riding accident the year after we met and was in a wheelchair after that. She inspired me to change careers and go back to school. Luckily, I had a double major at the university before and had taken many pre-med classes because I liked studying biology, so going back wasn't hard Then I went to medical school and specialized in orthopedic surgery because I wanted to learn how to fix the damage to Graciela's legs so she could walk again. I spent the rest of my twenties in school and residency learning my new profession.

Valeria complained bitterly about my going back to school and not having the time to travel with her and support her career. She wanted to leave Graciela with a nanny or send her to boarding school so we could travel together anywhere her career took us, to Europe, to Asia, to the United States. She said she couldn't stand to be around her daughter now that she was a cripple. As a dancer, she said it was especially difficult to look at Graciela's legs now. I was flabbergasted and I refused to go away with her and that was the beginning of the end of our marriage that only lasted three years. When we divorced, Graciela stayed with me, and Valeria and I were both happy with that arrangement. At least we could agree on something at the end."

"Oh, Noé, that's an incredible story. A surgeon! You are a surgeon. Wait a minute. Why are you working as a custodian at the junior college? What are you thinking?"

"Ellie, I'm an immigrant who has to start over to get licensed here. I must study for a multitude of tests to prove that my credentials were earned, not just given. I've been studying the manuals that go with each test. That's why I moved here from Mexico City. Graciela is studying at the National University at home in Mexico and very proud to be on her own. I knew I needed to get here to improve my English and try to find tutors and study groups to begin to prep for these exams. Graciela wants to go to graduate school here in Texas, so I'm trying to get things set up by getting licensed to be a doctor here. I just have a long way to go unfortunately."

"Noé, that explains so much about your English and manners and gentlemanly ways. You surely aren't from Texas though the men here often open doors for me and they all call me ma'am. I have to say that Texans are more mannerly than the New Yorkers I'm more familiar with lately. Maybe I can help you prepare for your exams. I don't have the medical or science background you do, but I can help you organize things and develop better study strategies. That is, if you want me to," Ellie said and looked searchingly at Noé for his reaction, wondering if she'd overstepped.

"I would love to have you help me, *mi amor*. Now, enough talking. Let's just relax here and enjoy the fire," Noé said as he used his finger to tip Ellie's face up to his so he could give her another kiss. He tentatively kissed her softly and when she reciprocated, ran his tongue along her lips until they parted. Soon, they were kissing deeply and Noé reached over to put his hand on Ellie's breast which caused her to gasp but not to stop their kiss or move his hand away from her breast. Encouraged, Noé rubbed his finger over her nipple till he felt it peak inside her bra. Then, he slipped his hand under her blouse and up to her breast and he gently grabbed it through the lace cup of her bra and gave the nipple a gentle tug.

Ellie moaned and leaned closer to Noé, wanting him to know she approved of what he had started. Their kiss intensified and then they were leaning back on the sofa and Noé slid over on top of Ellie and slowly rubbed his erection against her. Ellie accommodated him by spreading her legs, so he was pushing against her most sensitive spot. Noé pulled back and Ellie made a sound of disappointment but then moaned again when she felt him touch her intimately with his fingers.

"Noé, I want you closer. That feels so good. I want more," Ellie managed to gasp.

"Let me take off your clothes, *mi amor*. I want you too," Noé said as he sat up and quickly unbuttoned his shirt and then took off his belt and unbuttoned his pants. Ellie followed suit and took off her blouse and unsnapped her jeans. Suddenly shy, she looked up at Noé who had gotten up to take off his pants. She noticed his boots on the floor and couldn't really remember when he'd taken them off, but when she saw him take off his boxers, she swallowed the lump in her throat and stood to take off her bra and panties.

Noé took Ellie's hands in his and brought one up to his mouth and kissed the palm of one of her hands. Then he framed her face with his hands and kissed her again, pulling her close to his body. Ellie felt his erection against her stomach and wrapped her arms around Noé's waist and pressed her breasts against his chest enjoying the feel of his chest against her nipples.

She felt Noé's hand move between their bodies and his fingers come between her legs as he teased his way through her curls.

When he touched her sensitive skin, Ellie jumped at the sensation that felt almost foreign to her. It had been so many years since she'd been with a man.

Almost reflexively, she reached for his erection, and was rewarded with Noé's intake of breath, an indication to her that he was just as affected as she was. She stroked up and down the length of him and circled his penis at the base and then worked her way up, stroking his heavy erection till she got to the head, and ran her thumb over the drop of precum that was sitting there. Ellie was momentarily mesmerized by the slick feel of the cum on the head of his penis as she ran her thumb around the head several more times till Noé reached for her hand and said,

"*No más, querida*. (No more, sweetheart.) Not now. It's been too long for me. I want us to enjoy being together a little longer. This is too soon to end this moment together."

Noé turned and sat and pulled Ellie down on the couch with him. She noticed that he'd pulled the blanket down from the top edge of the sofa for them to lie down on. It was so soft that Ellie was mentally telling herself she was crazy to be thinking about the blanket that had to be either cashmere or alpaca in this exact moment. Soon, Noé covered Ellie's body with his and began to move back and forth on her, his penis rubbing against her clit, sending shockwaves through her long dormant body that was definitely no longer thinking about cashmere.

'Christ. My vibrator never feels this good. I may die right now just from the feelings he's giving me.'

"Noé, that's so good. That feels so good," Ellie managed to say as she moaned her satisfaction.

"Wait, *mi amor*. I want to make it feel even better. I need to be inside you now, Ellie. Are you ready for me?"
"Yes, Noé! Yes. Now!" Ellie said and waited impatiently while Noé opened a condom packet with his teeth and rolled the condom over himself and then slowly put the head of his dick inside her vagina. He held himself back, not wanting to hurt her with his eagerness, but Ellie took that decision away when she wrapped her legs around his butt and pulled him into her, deep.

For a moment both were still as they savored their intimate connection and then both began to move in perfect rhythm. It was over all too soon and both lay limply against each other.

Dios mío, Ellie. I don't know what to say, but I don't remember sex being that good though it's been a while."

"You just took the words out of my mouth. I don't remember sex being that good either. I think I may need a moment right now to recover though, if that's OK?"

Noé laughed and moved off her to take care of the condom and then said, "Do you think you can wake up enough to go take a shower with me?"

Images of a naked Noé ran through Ellie's mind and she decided she did have the energy to get in the shower with him. It sounded like a sinful pleasure that she couldn't wait to do. Ellie took Noé's offered hand and stood up. They went down the hall and around a corner into what had to be the master suite. It had a huge bed that they bypassed as Noé led her to the shower. She noted in the back of her mind that the lights must be on some sort of motion sensor because dim lighting had come on when they walked into the room. She'd have to ask him about that later.

But right now, the shower was the main event as far as Ellie was concerned. She couldn't wait to be body to body in the shower with Noé who had a body like an athlete that reminded her of statues in a museum though that did sound corny to her as she thought it.

The warm water cascaded down on them from the double shower heads as well as the jets on the wall. Noé put some liquid body wash in his palm and then proceeded to wash Ellie's body, starting with her breasts. He kissed her tenderly while he tweaked her breasts after he'd lathered them up. He turned her toward the shower stream of water that washed of the soap and took one nipple in his mouth and sucked, using little pressure. When Ellie moaned and leaned into him, he sucked the entire areola into his mouth, tonguing the nipple.

Ellie responded by reaching down and running her hand up and down his erect penis once again. She took the bottle of body wash, put some in her palm and then thoroughly washed his penis which became even more engorged with her attention. When Noé would have reached for her hand, Ellie pushed his hands away and sat down on the bench behind her which put his penis at right about the perfect height to take in her mouth. She closed her lips around his cock and began to suck him, her tongue putting pressure on the sensitive spot on the underside of the head.

Noé moaned and put his hand on the wall behind her to steady himself while Ellie continued to stroke and suck him simultaneously. He couldn't stop the rhythm his body started as he thrust himself further into her mouth, the action mimicking the sex act. Ellie could feel that Noé was getting close as she tasted more precum on her tongue, its saltiness not unpleasant. Everything about this man was wonderful, even his cum in her mouth. At the last moment, Noé pulled out and shot stream after stream of cum on the wall to be washed off by the shower jets. Ellie just sat there; her head leaned against his stomach as she slowly came out of the intensely sexual moment. Even though the climax had been his, Ellie had enjoyed every minute of bringing Noé to climax, an act she'd avoided before because she hadn't really liked the thought of doing that for Chad.

When Noé recovered, he washed Ellie all over with the handheld shower, getting all the soap off her body and then his. He turned off the shower, both strangely silent, for them, as both always had so much to say. He wrapped Ellie in a big, luxurious bath towel and then wrapped another around himself and motioned for her to dry off as he was. With a smile and a nod of his head to follow him, Noé left the bathroom and went to the big king-size bed and laid down.

"Come join me, *querida* (sweetheart). I want to hold you."

"I'd like that, Noé. Please hold me," Ellie said as she settled in the bed beside him. They both must have dozed a while because Ellie awoke to the feel of Noé softly kissing her breast and then the sensation that his hand made as it trailed down over her stomach to her pussy. He separated the curls and then the folds and found her clit which he began to carefully stroke watching her face throughout.

"Noé, I'm so sensitive, I'm going to come right away. You make me feel so good. I don't know when I've ever felt this good. Oh," Ellie said as Noé stroked her clit with firmer pressure and when she felt her body start to shudder with another orgasm, he put two fingers inside of her and pressed inside of her womb and she shrieked with the increased intensity of her orgasm.

Noé withdrew his hand from her pussy and got up to bring a warm, damp cloth to wipe her off while Ellie watched unbelieving. This whole scenario was so different from what she'd been used to with Chad. It was so intimate, but very tender and caring.

Noé soon returned from the bathroom where he'd gone to drop off the washcloth and lay down on the bed, wrapping his arms around her, nuzzling her neck with small kisses. Now, tell me, *mi amor*, do you want another nap, or should we raid the kitchen? Either would be fine with me," he said with a smile in his voice.

"Much as I'd like to just go to sleep with you in this super cozy position, I think we ought to raid the kitchen. I'm hungry as well as exhausted. This has been quite the first date, Mr. Vásquez. Quite unexpected."

Laughing, Noé got up and pulled Ellie up to her feet and kissed her on the forehead and then turned to lead her back to the kitchen. As they made their way through the darkened hallways, Ellie was glad he was leading her as this house was cavernous. She wondered what it looked like in the light of day. She hoped that she'd find out.

Chapter 4: First Day

Monday morning rolled around all too soon for Ellie and she awoke with a cold tongue on her cheek. She managed to open one eye and saw Duke sitting beside her bed, his tongue lolling out the side of his mouth. He looked at her for a moment and then woofed at her, as if to say it was past time to get up.

Ellie got up, looked at the clock and was relieved to see she had plenty of time for a shower. She could even wash and blow dry her hair rather than twisting it up into a ponytail like she usually did. Getting quickly dressed, Ellie went to the kitchen and found Flo bustling around and putting a cup of coffee in front of her.

"OK, girl. What's your pleasure? Carbs or protein? I mean pancakes or eggs? You have time for either."

"If you wouldn't mind, I'd like what you gave me last time. A couple of pancakes here and then your version of an egg and muffin sandwich to take along with me plus some coffee in my travel mug to go along with it. Have I told you lately how much I love you, Auntie Flo?

"Yes, dear. Every day. You know it's no trouble and I'm hoping that while you make yourself and sandwich or a snack for later, you'll tell me more about your date with Noé. We hardly got to talk this weekend with situating your new house and cleaning every visible surface. Back to your date. He is quite the hunk. I can see why you're so attracted to him."

"Hey, wait a minute, Flo. Don't get carried away. We had a really nice time together Saturday night and enjoyed the Mexican rodeo and the mariachi music very much. Is that what you wanted to hear?"

"You know that it's not. I'm waiting for details about the sex. You didn't come in till three a.m., so I know there's more to this story," Flo said and looked expectantly at her niece.

"You are worse than my girlfriends back in college always wanting all the details. Sex was wonderful and I'm happy to announce that I haven't forgotten how to do it. Satisfied?"

"I knew it! I knew you'd fall for this guy. Is he a keeper? When do you go out next with him?"

"Whoa, Flo. Slow down. We've just been out once. Let's see where this goes, OK?" Ellie said with a little exasperation in her voice. Relenting, she said, "I hope it does go somewhere though, auntie, because he's really a dreamy man. I want to get to know him more and spend more time with him and not just for the sex. He makes me laugh and feel special and cherished."

"Well, it's about time. That bozo Chad had years to make you feel like that and never did. I think this man has made you feel things you've wanted for a long time. What woman wouldn't? I'm happy for you, niece," Flo said smiling as she put two pancakes on Ellie's plate on the counter, took the syrup out of the microwave, and pushed the butter over towards Ellie.

After breakfast, Ellie gave both Flo and Duke a hug and then went out to her car, carrying her coffee and egg sandwich, anxious to get to work and get the first day with students started. She pulled into the faculty parking and walked toward her building. Rounding the corner, she saw Noé standing by her door, propped against the wall with a bouquet of daisies in his hand. He quickly kissed her, gave her a brief one-armed hug and then pushed the daisies her way.

"I've got to go get busy, *querida*, but I just wanted you to know I was thinking about you."

"Oh, Noé, thank you. Daisies are my favorite. How did you know?"

"Your aunt likes me and gave me the inside information. I'm glad you like them." He gave her another quick kiss and then left, walking briskly down the hall.

Smiling, Ellie unlocked her office and then dropped things on her desk and went to look under the sink for a vase for her flowers. Finding one and filling it with water, she put her flowers in and set the vase on her desk.

'I can't remember when I've been given flowers. Chad the Cad never did sweet things like that. Tricky of him to have called my aunt to find out about my favorite flowers. Very thoughtful.'

Ellie's musings were cut short by the door opening and her two teachers walking in.

"Well, what a nice surprise! You're early. Well done."

Both Trace and Courtney had chagrined and somewhat hesitant looks on their faces, knowing they hadn't made a good impression last week. Independently, they had decided to come in early to try to do better this time around and were pleased that Ellie noticed and praised them.

"OK. Let's get to our rooms. Each of you take your rosters and a stack of placement tests. Remember that if someone can't even begin the test, just place them in the basic class without making a big production of it. We don't want to embarrass anyone today and make them quit before they even get started. When they finish, let them look through some of the *National Geographics* each of you has in your room. From what I've heard, some of our students will sign up today for the first time, being new to us but former high school dropouts. At least I hope that's what's going to happen."

"Er, Ellie, how do you know this?" Trace asked curiously.

"Well, I went to meet with someone who works here that I hoped had connections with the Black community here in town and around the area. We had a good talk, and he said he'd help me. I'm trying to recruit in the Hispanic community also."

"Er, why would you do that? Isn't it better for us if we don't have very many students?" Trace asked seriously.

'Geez, this guy is either a real asshole or just stupid.' "Well, Trace, this program is all about the students and improving their lives and job opportunities, not about us. Does that make sense?"

"Um, yes, Ellie. I guess I'm just nervous about today and thought it'd be easier to help people if we didn't have very many students. Sorry. I must have sounded like a jerk."

"Well, you did, but your explanation helps me to understand your comment better. Today's going to be a good day, so let's get ready," Ellie said with a smile.

The bell rang for their first class, and a few people hesitantly stuck their heads inside the door to Ellie's room. She welcomed them and checked their names off the rosters. Trace and Courtney each took their students to their rooms to get started with testing.

Ellie looked up in surprise when she heard Noé call her name. "Ah, Mr. Vasquez. Can I help you?"

"I've brought you a few students who were lost," he said as he turned to them and spoke in rapid Spanish and then with a smile, turned to go.

"Thank you, Mr. Vasquez," Ellie called after him and turned to four new students. After adding their names, she asked them in Spanish about their educational levels and found they'd gone through six years of school but had not graduated and wanted GEDs and to learn English.

It felt good to be back into the rhythm of school Ellie found as the morning progressed. About 11, Mr. Jenkins stuck his head in the open door and called out to her.

"Hi, Mr. Jenkins. It's good to see you. Can I help you?"

"Come on in, now y'all. Don't give this lady any sass or I'll deal with you myself. Understood?" Mr. Jenkins said as he stepped aside to let in a group of six African American men in their late teens and early twenties.

"Thank you! Mr. Jenkins. Now, gentlemen, why don't you come over here and take a seat so I can get your names, and we can get started. It's really nice to see you here today."

Looking at the doorway to check to see if Davis Jenkins was still there, the young men sat down, some more reluctantly than others. Their seeming leader spoke up first.

"Er, Ms. Thompson, Davis came to us to tell us this GED class would be different from the ones before and different from our high school. Both of those sucked. How are you different?" he asked sullenly.

"Well, Mr. . . your name, please?"

"Leroy Brown."

"Oh, I like your name. You're much too young to know about a song from when I was young about a man named Leroy Brown." Seeing the blank look on his face, she continued, "But I digress. You have a valid concern and question, Mr. Brown. Let me tell you how," Ellie said and looked at their sullen faces to see if she'd broken the ice. *'Nope, still an iceberg and holding.'*

"I'm going to start by giving you placement tests so we can start your programs exactly where you need to be. There won't be any time wasted going over old stuff you already know. I've done this before, Mr. Brown, with adult students and with high school students who had dropped out that I brought back to school and helped them catch up. If you're willing to work, I'm willing to teach you what you need to pass the GED. I expect you to be here every day and to work hard while you're here. There's no homework because I know that adult students have a life outside this classroom. Some of you have families to support and have jobs to go to even though you may want a better job. Getting your GED will open doors for you in employment and if you want to continue your education at a community or junior college or get into a trade school program, you'll have what you need for the next step. OK?"

There was no response. Nothing. Complete quiet. Ellie almost wished they'd start their surly comment again. She stared at them, and they stared at her. There was a noise at the door and then Courtney came into the room. Then there was sound. The wrong kind. Whistles and catcalls started.

"Courtney, I'll come see you in a minute. Please go back to your room." Ellie said in a controlled voice and turned to look at her class of currently obnoxious men.

"I see I forgot to tell you about myself, gentlemen. I taught in public school for seventeen years, most of those in high school and I was an assistant principal for three and the associate principal at a high school of 2600 students for the last five years. Oh, I also raised four kids. The last thing I'm going to put up with is a bunch of rowdy children in my classroom. Your choice. Act like gentlemen or go home. You decide right now whether you want to change your lives for the better because I'm not going to put up with your crap. Oh, I'm going to call Ms. Jones back in here so you can make an apology to her for disrespecting here like you just did. We're not on a playground in middle school, gentlemen. You are deciding today and right now if you really mean it when you say you want to make a better life for yourself and your families. It's up to you, not me. Just so we're clear, I get paid whether you're here or not. I'd rather you were here, but I'm too old to be disrespected by students who don't act like men and choose to act like boys. Clear?"

Leroy looked at her and then at his group. The rest of them clearly looked to him to make the decision. "All right. Understood, but I don't want to apologize."

"Well, then, you didn't understand. This is my classroom, and everyone respects everyone else. That means if someone gives an answer that sounds less than correct and thoughtful, no one laughs. Learning involves mistakes and laughing at someone trying to learn just isn't cool, correct or acceptable. Maybe I'll teach you your first words today: benevolent dictator. That means I'm the law in this room. No questions. Benevolent means I'll be polite and kind and maybe even come to like you as a person. But please focus on the dictator part of that term I just wrote on the board. Now, can we get on with this and move forward? We're wasting time we don't have to waste to get you guys caught up. Ready?"

Leroy just stared at Ellie, but she stared back till he nodded his head. She got out her cell and texted Courtney to come back. Courtney hesitantly walked back in the room, clearly apprehensive. "Yes, Ms. Thompson?"

Ellie just looked at Leroy who stood and nodded to his group to stand. "We want to apologize for disrespecting you when you came in before. That was wrong. I'm sorry," Leroy said, and his group mumbled the same.

Courtney looked shocked and then smiled, "Why, thank you. That means a lot to me. Er, I just came in to check to see when I could let my students go to lunch."

"Right now is fine. Be sure they all have campus maps and understand how to read them. At least one person from yours and Mr.Trace's class needs to know how to follow the map. I need to get my students registered first and then they'll be along too," Ellie said with a smile.

When she looked at her group, they seemed surprised. "OK. Why those looks? What is it?"

Leroy said, "We're not used to a teacher smiling at us, especially not after yelling at us."

"Well, first, I didn't yell. Did I? No raised voices here and there won't be unless we're playing a game and having fun. Also, I will always expect you to act correctly for me, but if you mess up, but apologize and accept responsibility for your mistake, then we move on. Each day is a new day. No grudges here. Just be positive and work hard and I'm happy with you. I don't like being a grump, but I will be if I need to. I prefer enjoying life and that includes this classroom. Now each of you fill out this form to the best of your knowledge and memory. Here's some pens; pass around the box, please."

Looking like they still weren't sure what was happening, Ellie's group quickly finished the registration forms and handed them in to her.

"OK, gentlemen, the morning session for GED is officially over. However, we didn't get as far as I'd hoped today, so if you have the time, I'd like you to stay another half hour so you can take the placement test. It's not too long and it's something we can do tomorrow if that's better for you. Your decision.

Nobody got up after looking at each other. "We're ready if you are, Ms. Thompson."

"That's wonderful! Here, each of you come get a test and work through it as far as you can. If you must skip some questions, that's OK. Just keep on till you reach the end,' Ellie said with a smile, her heart warmed that her cranky, sullen bunch of young men had completely changed their attitudes.

The half hour passed and one by one they finished the test and brought it to her desk. "Thank you for doing this, gentlemen. I'm proud of you today. You showed me and yourselves that you're serious about getting more education. See you tomorrow and have a good rest of the day."

They all nodded at her, and some said, "Goodbye" as they left her room.

About fifteen minutes later, Ellie was sitting at her desk, eating the lunch Auntie

Flo had packed for her when she heard a knock at the door and looked up to see Davis Jenkins. "Come in, Mr. Jenkins. You caught me eating at my desk. Teacher hazard, I guess," she said with a laugh.

"Well, you need to eat your lunch since you gave up half of it to test those rascals I brought you this morning. They came by to tell me about their first day. They said you yelled at them for being rude to one of the other teachers and you made them apologize. Oh, and that you would kick them out if they didn't act respectful to you and each other and the other teachers. I almost forgot, that you had a job and didn't need them to get paid, but if they wanted to get a better job, they needed you to help them get their GEDs. It was their choice. Your way or the highway. They said you sounded like the army or something but understood when you told them you'd been an assistant high school principal for 8 years. I'm impressed, Ms. Thompson."

"Please, Ellie. I think we're going to be friends, Mr. Jenkins. They seem to have very good memories because that's exactly what happened. Once they knew I was serious, they settled down. I was impressed that they didn't run out the door when they could, but stayed late to take the placement test that we didn't get to while sorting out attitudes,"

"I'm impressed that you gave up half your lunch hour on students that came in causing trouble and didn't send for me to chew them out."

"Ah, if I couldn't handle them myself, where would we be? I think you have too much to do running your staff to babysit my students though I do appreciate your support. As I told them, respect is the key and no grudges."

Davis Jenkins looked intently at Ellie and finally nodded his head and said, "You'll do, Miss Ellie, you'll do just fine."

"Well, I thank you, sir. I'm glad you approve and look forward to getting and keeping as many students as we can round up back on track. It'll be fun to see them turn around. Yes?" Ellie said with a smile as he turned to go.

Almost on his heels, Trace and Courtney came in and Courtney said, "How did you manage those guys that were here before? They were something else."

"Well, they wanted to be difficult at first because they haven't had many positive learning experiences, but after we had a little talk, they came around and even stayed after to take the placement tests. I respect that. As

I told them, each day is a new day. No grudges."

"Well, I hope I don't get any difficult students. I'll be running to find you if I do, Ellie. I couldn't believe it when Courtney told me they all apologized to her and were very polite. Impressive."

"They're going to be a good bunch. How were your students? Did you get all the placement tests done?"

"Yes, and everybody could finish the tests. The Spanish speaking students you talked to first did the best actually. Two of them tested out of the math," Trace said with a surprised expression.

"This is what we talked about last week. Some students have very good backgrounds because they didn't have interrupted education and six years in many countries prepares them for most of the GED content. All they'll need is fine tuning on their English and their accents. They'll learn quickly," Ellie explained to her staff, pleased that both had handled their mornings so well. "Good job, crew. I'm glad the morning went so well."

The afternoon group was small, and Ellie had her staff do the testing while she worked on grading the morning's placement tests.

She'd just finished when Dave Morris walked in.

"Hi, Ellie. How'd it go today? I see you've got a stack of tests. Looks like we had a good turnout."

Yes, and I had some help recruiting some new ones that weren't on our rosters. We added almost a dozen students to our rosters."

"A dozen?! That's amazing and will increase our funding, which is always good news. How did you accomplish that?" Dave asked quizzically.

"When we went over our rosters last week, I noticed that all the students who had signed up were white and I figured in a town like this with three major groups represented, I needed to reach out the African American and Hispanic communities because I knew from studying the state report card that our local high school had dropouts in all three groups. It was successful and I was glad to see some more faces today. I hoped you would be too," Ellie said looking at Dave.

"Yes. Yes. I don't know why no one thought of reaching out before. I think the previous director and teachers thought this program was like *Field of Dreams* and students would just appear here. Good thinking, Ellie. I'm glad you walked in here last week. You're good for the program already. You've made some fundamental positive changes and somehow gotten your two teachers in shape which is the most amazing part."

"Someday I'll tell you about that. For now. I'm glad we're off to a good start. We might even get some more students once the word gets out. If they don't show up now, they'll come in for the next block of classes. Oh, I have a question. Do we put PSAs on the radio station in town? That might help bring some more students in too."

"Radio station? Oh, you mean that one on the corner on the town square, across from the courthouse?"

"That's the one. I think they play Tejano music so that would reach some of our demographic. I'll try to stop by and check it out in the next few days. Also, do we put anything in the local paper? It's been around since the late 1880's and still going strong. Also, there's an outreach group in town I should talk to. I'm hoping you'll OK all this. Right?"

"Of course, Ellie. I wish someone had thought of all your ideas before. Our program has been limping along for years, and nobody ever tried to move it forward.

Again, thanks for applying for this job. OK. I'm on my way around campus checking on other departments. I just wanted to stop by and say 'hi' and get your opinion of day #1."

"It was all good. Bye, Dave. See you soon," Ellie said smiling.

After finishing the tests and setting up some computer assignments for some of the new students, Ellie went to find Trace and Courtney and told them to go home and rest their feet.

"How did you know?!" Courtney said.

"Because I have the same teacher feet and did for years. If you're spending your time moving around checking on your students, your feet will bother you till they get in shape. Sitting behind a desk is no way to teach. You will find how much faster you get to know your students' strengths and weaknesses by looking over their shoulders. Some are shy and won't ask for help even if they need it. Others just don't have the habit of calling attention to themselves in an area where they lack confidence in their skills. See you guys tomorrow. Good job today, by the way."

Beaming at the praise that they knew they'd earned, Trace and Courtney left walking much slower than they'd started out in the morning.

'Ah, even the young get tired. Glad it's not just my middle-aged self. Uh, wait a minute. Almost middle-aged.' Hearing a knock, Ellie looked up to see Noé standing in the doorway smiling at her.

"Noé! It's so good to see you. Are you here to walk me out today? I'm tired and ready to go. It was a busy, productive day."

"I hear there was some drama in the morning, but you came out on top."

"Geez, word travels fast here. It was nothing I couldn't handle, and I think the students and I reached an understanding, and they'll be back tomorrow ready to work. They even stayed after to take the placement test we never got do because we were dealing with their attitude issues. I like and respect that."

"Well, I have it on authority that you're a badass who doesn't put up with shit from anyone," Noé said with smile.

"Honestly, I don't know what to say to that. Thank you?" Ellie said laughing.

"I'm on break now but won't get off till 4:30. Do you have plans for tonight? I'd like to see you, Ellie."

"At the risk of bringing trouble into an evening, are you up to seeing my Aunt Flo again? You can come over for dinner tonight if you'd like. I'd like to see you too."

"Aunt Flo? I might have said I wasn't sure two days ago, but since she gave me the flowers tip, I think we're OK. Dinner would be nice unless you'd like me to take you both out to eat."

"Another time. I'm a little tired from today and a quiet, no fuss evening at home sounds really good about now. All right?"

"It's a date. What time?" Noé asked, pleased that he'd be seeing Ellie again so soon.

"Six o'clock. Bye now, Noé. I don't want you to see me limping out of here on my sore feet."

"I'll just have to pretend I'm not watching because I'm walking you out to your car," Noé said firmly.

"Ah, bossy already? Alright, let's go. I think your carrying my book bag today will help me be able to get out of here on my own two feet. Here," Ellie laughed and packed the last of her things in her bag and handed it to Noé as she got up and groaned a little.

On the way home, Ellie called Flo on her phone hookup in her car, "Flo, I've invited company to dinner. Is that alright? If we don't have enough, tell me now and I'll swing by the HEB grocery on my way home. Tell me quickly though because I'm almost there."

"If the company is Noé, then he's welcome and we have enough. If it's not him, then 'no' and you need to cook."

"So that's the way it's going to be? Oh, that doesn't sound fair. You're playing favorites now are you? I'm glad you like him. I do too," Ellie said, happy that her only and much-loved relative of her parents' generation in her life approved of her new friend. *'Friend seems a bit mild since I hopped into bed with him two nights ago on our first date of all things. Boyfriend seems like too young a word, so I guess I don't really know what we are. We'll figure that out later. I just want to see him again.'*

Just before six, Flo and Ellie heard a knock at the door, and both started to get it. Hurrying, Flo said, "You might as well just let me get it. I want to see your young man again too."

"Auntie Flo, you sound like a 'geezer' with that 'your young man' comment. Have you been reading *Little House on the Prairie* lately?"

"No and be quiet. He'll hear us and turn around and leave," Flo said as she got to the door and then opened it with a beaming smile on her face.

"Noé, it's so nice to see you! Come in," Flo said, holding the door wide.

Noé put a bouquet of flowers in her hands and held the other out for Ellie.

"Noé, you shouldn't have. You already gave me flowers today. How sweet," Ellie said as she smelled the fragrance of her bouquet.

"Flowers! Noé I can't remember when I've been given flowers. That's very nice of you, young man," Flo said smiling broadly as she turned to go to the kitchen to put her flowers in a vase.

She left the room and Noé and Ellie moved towards each other. Loosely holding Ellie so as not to crush her flowers, Noé softly kissed her and stepped back, happy to be there for dinner with the two women. He knew tonight would be fun and interesting. Aunt Flo was a character, and Ellie was already special to him even though they were moving fast.

'Not dating seriously for years hasn't prepared me for Ellie. We're moving so fast, but it feels right. Nothing feels rushed. I feel like I've known her forever. I'm glad we met and we're spending time together. It feels even better that her aunt seems to like me. Family is important and matters to Ellie as well as to me.'

After dinner, they sat down in the living room with glasses of tea. "That was a really good meal. I can't remember when I've had such a good home-cooked meal actually," Noé said looking at both Ellie and Flo.

"Aunt Flo's the one to take credit for that meal. She's always watching a cooking show or taking a new cooking class."

"Why, thank you Noé. Ellie's right. I do like to learn new dishes and tonight's was one from an online class I took last spring. I'd been waiting for someone new to try it out. I'm glad you liked it," Flo said, pleased by Noé's comments.

'Why couldn't she have met someone like this to marry all those years ago instead of Chad the Cad? What a piece of garbage! She did acquire his four kids out of that though and I do love them.' Flo mused as she compared the man sitting across from her. *'He is certainly handsome, and Ellie loves Spanish which he speaks fluently. He's a gentleman, too. I'm going to be hopeful here that they continue to discover each other and grow this new relationship.'*

"Well, I'll let you two alone to talk or watch a movie. I'm glad you came to dinner tonight, Noé. It was nice getting to know you better," Flo said as she stood to go to her room.'

"Flo, don't feel like you have to go. Please stay with us," Noé said as he looked at Ellie and smiled at them both.

"Yes, Flo. Stay and we'll watch a movie. We'll have a movie night. Really, it's OK," Ellie added her comments to Noé's."

"Thank you. Really. I'm a little tired though and want to get comfy to read the new book I got at the library today," Flo said as she continued down the hall to her room.

"Noé, thank you. That was very sweet. I don't know many men who would invite my quirky aunt to stick around. Of course, you realize I don't know many men. Right?" Ellie said teasingly.

"Yes, *mi amor*. (my love) I meant it. Why not all of us hang around to watch TV or talk? Though I like being alone with you and possibly stealing some kisses, I like family time too."

Ellie scooted closer to Noé on the couch and turned her face to his. "I think I'd like you to steal a kiss about now. OK?"

Not waiting for more encouragement, Noé leaned over to Ellie and kissed her softly, tenderly. *'I want this to just be a kiss, not a prelude to sex which I will not have here on her living room couch with her aunt just down the hall. Though I think I might want to regardless of Flo.'*

136

What started out as a soft kiss soon turned into a deeper one, Noé's best intentions evaporating as they moved closer. Finally stopping for breath, both Ellie and Noé sat and looked in each other's eyes, breathing heavily.

"What is it with us?! One kiss and I'm ready to kiss you all night long. My long dry spell must have made me sex-crazed or sex-starved. I promise I've never been like this Noé. I've never slept with a man on the first date, and I've never felt like I can't keep my hands off someone like I feel with you. Don't just look at me like that. Tell me what you're thinking," Ellie commanded, frustrated with herself and with the unfamiliar feelings she was having.

"I don't know, Ellie. I've been so woman-averse after my wife's antics, and I was so busy with school and my residency and being a father to Graciela that I haven't had a serious relationship since my wife. I feel the same as you do right now. I even told myself that I would take things slowly tonight. That it wouldn't be about sex but about getting to know each other better because I want to know you, Ellie. I want to build a relationship with you. I hope I'm not rushing you, but we seem to be doing everything so fast and a little backwards. I wanted to tell you that though kissing you makes all my good intentions just evaporate."

"Me, too, Noé. I want to get to know you better too, I can't disagree that we're going fast and backwards in a way, but I like where we're going, and I hope we continue the way we're going. I do have to say that I think talking about things is a logical next step, so let's try to do that. I want to learn more about Graciela. I can see she's very important to you."

Smiling broadly, Noé began to talk about his daughter. "First, I have to say that I think it's interesting that we both have children in our lives that mean so much that we aren't related to by blood. It doesn't matter though, does it? Graciela and I got along well from the beginning. I think she was happy to have a parent who wanted to spend time with her and consider her best interests. If I'd been around that day she was injured, she never would have ridden that horse and had her riding accident.

"I think Valeria felt guilty about not spending any time with Graciela. She had just returned from a two-month European tour and was trying to ease her guilty conscience because we'd had a fight about her lack of involvement in her daughter's life the night before. I was happily the stay-at-home parent, but I felt that Graciela needed her mother as well. Valeria, of course, disagreed.

"However, when I left for my shift at the civil engineering center, she went to find her daughter and asked her what she wanted to do that day. Graciela loved riding, so she told her mother she wanted to go to the stables. When we got there, her regular trainer was busy, so Valeria asked one of the grooms what horses were available. He walked her down the stall rows and when they passed Roca's stall, Valeria told the groom that it was the horse her daughter would ride that day.

"The groom protested, saying that Roca had just gotten back from touring the show circuit and needed a little down time before he was ridden again. He needed pasture turn out, not a ride in the ring. Valeria insisted as she always did, wanting to have her way in everything. Even Graciela, who was fearless around horses, could see that Roca wasn't in the right frame of mind for a ride that day. She said so to Valeria who brushed aside her concerns and those of the groom and insisted that Roca was the most beautiful horse there, the most magnificent and the only one fitting for her daughter.

"Well, you know this didn't end well because Roca exploded when they got to the riding ring. Unfortunately, my daughter was on his back by then. He looked like a rodeo horse and finally reared up and went over backward with Graciela under him. Her legs were crushed with his weight.

"I was at the office near the end of my shift when my boss came to get me to tell me that my daughter was in the ER with very serious injuries. I ran to my car though I don't remember driving to the ER and found Valeria in a trance, mumbling "That horse needs to be shot. That horse needs to be shot."

"Graciela looked so small on the bed; her face streaked with tears. She looked up at me and said, 'Daddy, will I be OK?'

"I had to tell her I didn't know, but we would do everything possible to make that so. She hugged me as she continued to softly cry. Finally, Valeria's ramblings got on my nerves, and I told her to shut up and let the doctors tell us what would happen next.

"The doctor had called in an orthopedic surgeon to consult, and he said the easiest solution would be amputation. I told him to go and started calling other surgeons to come consult. Valeria was useless, which I'm glad about because she would have just said to amputate to be able to walk away and start another tour.

"Finally, on the fourth consult, the surgeon said he could stabilize her legs now and that after seeing how they healed, could do more surgery later while she was also doing physical therapy. That was the doctor I chose to work on my daughter because he offered the best hope. He said they were experimenting with new procedures that could help her and that more discoveries were so close. He gave us hope and as a result I started a new career path.

"Valeria opposed my career change, of course, but we were rich. She'd made millions from her touring and could afford for me to return to school and study. She complained bitterly about how having to have Graciela around was bad for her mental health because she couldn't concentrate on her new routines. Graciela's legs made her sick to her stomach, and she couldn't stand being around her own daughter.

"I told her she was going to pay for my schooling and a separate residence for Graciela and me and that we were getting a divorce with Graciela coming with me. I would have sole custody, and Valeria never had to worry about her own mental anguish again. I tell you these things calmly and dispassionately now, but our discussions were anything but calm. They were shouting matches, long, drawn-out verbal battles. I tried to keep them away from Graciela because no child should ever have to hear that their mother doesn't want them. I don't think I succeeded in sheltering her enough though. She had always had a distant relationship with her mother because Valeria had Graciela constantly away at a boarding school of some kind.

"However, after this, she became bitter about her mother and her self-esteem suffered too. It was an uphill battle to turn my cynical, surly daughter back into the sweet little girl I first met. I'm not sure I have completely because sometimes I still see that shell-shocked, rejected little girl in her comments and interactions with people. It's her armor, the shell that protects her from rejection."

"How awful! It seems we have more in common than I knew. I also became a parent because my ex's kids' mom didn't want them or their dad. The last part I could understand because I ended up not wanting him either. I thought that it never happened, that a mother would so easily abandon her kids. Horrible!" Ellie commiserated with Noé, disgust on her face as she recalled her situation with Chad and her first moments with his kids.

"Ellie, *te tengo mucha confianza*, I trust you; I haven't told that story of my past to anyone and I hope to never again. It brings up so many bad thoughts of hard times, horrible times for me and Graciela. If it's not too hard, tell me about your children."

"It's not a hard story like yours, but it doesn't show a good example of motherhood. When Chad and I started dating, he treated me so well, but now I think he was just shopping for someone to help with his four kids. I didn't even know he had four kids till we got engaged six months later. He was a master at redirecting conversations where he wanted them to go and knew how to romance me to keep me focused only on the here and now. I was just stupid. We've been divorced for ten years and we were only married for five, but once I found out about his kids and got to know them, I fell in love with them.

"They were so prickly at the beginning because they were dealing with their mother's rejection. She had checked out of their lives for quite a while, and the divorce was just a formality at the end. It turns out that Chad was still married when we started dating and was just finalizing his divorce when we got engaged. I never knew any of this till later.

It took a few months of putting up with the snotty obnoxiousness of his kids before they came around. Once they figured out that I was there for them, was going to show up at their sports events, at school and to take them to the dentist and all those normal things, their attitudes got better. They are stair steps in age, only a year apart. When I met them, they were eleven, ten, nine and eight years old. I was their mom for five years and when Chad and I split, he was awarded custody because he was their biological parent, and I was only the stepmom. However, the one good thing Chad did was listen to his kids and let them live with me most of the time. It freed up his time for playing around with more women, and he didn't have to listen to his kids complaining to him what an asshole he'd been. I was thrilled to be able to keep the kids with me and we're still in contact though they're grown now. Even the youngest is twenty-three and just graduated from college. I'm so proud of them all," Ellie said and sighed as she remembered those times.

"You should be proud. It sounds like they were lucky to have you in their lives after

their mother abandoned them and being
stuck with Chad the Cad. Do I have that
name right? Your Aunt Flo told me that was
his name," Noé laughed and reached over to
run his knuckles over Ellie's cheek.

Ellie leaned into his hand and closed her
eyes, happy that they were together, and
each knew more about the other and the
important events in their lives that had made
them who they were today.

"Do you mind telling me why you and
Chad broke up, Ellie? If not, that's OK with
me," Noé hurried to add as he didn't want to
push her to bring up a painful past even if
she wasn't ready.

"I don't mind, and I'd rather just be done
with the whole story tonight and then forget
it for good, Noé. We were in our fifth year
of marriage, and I thought things were going
so well. The kids were happy and doing well
in school. There were no fights, no problems
that I knew of. Then one day, Chad came
home and said he wanted a divorce. I was
thunderstruck and asked him why. He said
that he'd fallen in love with Lacy at work,
his secretary, and wanted to make his life
with her. The oldest kids walked in from
sports practice and heard the last of his
words and were furious. Everybody started
yelling except me. I just sat there cold, in a

fog. I couldn't believe he wanted to take my children from me and end what I thought was our happy life.

"I came back to the present when the kids sat beside me on the couch and hugged me from each side. They kept telling him they weren't going with him no matter what he said or did. I was their mom, and they weren't losing me because he was being an asshole. When the younger two came home, the noise started over again. He packed up and left the house for I don't know where. When we were in court and the judge said the kids would go with their biological parent, I was destroyed. I sat there sobbing with the kids beside me and Aunt Flo behind for moral support.

"There is a happy ending to this though because once the kids went home with Chad, it only took a day before he called me and said they were mine if I still wanted them. Apparently, they'd made it their mission to make his life a living hell. I said to send them over right then and they would always have a home with me. Aunt Flo stayed with me through this, and I really needed her then. I was so happy when the kids came back, and we could settle into our normal lives again."

"I'm glad he was at least smart enough to see that his kids needed you back in their lives. I'm happy for you to have had all those years with them in your house. Could I ask why you never had children with Chad? Did you already have too many to take care of? Again, forget it if it's too hard to talk about," Noé said as he held her hand and brought it to his lips to kiss.

"Uh, yes, this is painful because my greatest dream was to have a child that I carried in my womb. I believe in adoption wholeheartedly and that family is can be blood related though not all family is by blood. After the first year, we went to several fertility specialists. Chad said that his sperm were great, but my womb was an "inhospitable environment," that I would never conceive. He reminded me he'd already fathered four children so that made sense. I went through the hormone shots and everything else but finally gave up trying. It was just too depressing every month to take the pregnancy tests and find that once again I hadn't conceived. It made me feel like a failure and I got tired of his phony, consoling words. He didn't sound like he meant them after a while, and he complained about the money being wasted and my mood swings with all those hormone shots. It was a disaster but as he reminded me, I had his four children to take care of already and I should be grateful for that. After the first visit, Chad handled all the communications with the doctors because I was too depressed and just couldn't face reading all those reports repeatedly saying that I was a failure as a woman. It was a hard time in my life, Noé," Ellie said as a tear silently streaked down her cheek.

"Ah, *mi amor.* Don't be sad. He was right about one thing and that you had four kids that loved you in your life. I'm glad you had them to mother and raise. With your love and compassion, you're a natural mother. If we continue seeing each other, which I hope we do, I'm going to add another child to your list of kids who need your attention. Graciela will be here in another month or less to start her graduate program at UT in Austin."

"Will she be upset that we're seeing each other, Noé? I don't want to cause you problems with your daughter. That's the last thing I want our relationship to do," Ellie said, concerned about what Graciela might feel about her dad seeing a new woman.

"Well, I could say the same to you. What will your kids think about their mom dating the custodian at your school? They might not approve and might not want any man in your life to take your attention away from them," Noé pointed out.

"I think that's highly unlikely as they've been telling me for years that I need to get out there and date and find a new man. I think they'll be happy that I'm not alone. Even if they did, I'd tell them it's my business if I have someone new in my life," Ellie said and reminded Noé that he hadn't answered her question, "And you?"

"Same thing. Graciela says I need a new woman in my life and that's it's been way too long since I've dated anyone. She says I'm too boring because I don't do anything but go to work and work on my study."

"What study is that?" Ellie asked, intrigued. What kind of study could he be doing with his current job?

"Well, don't laugh; I know it sounds preposterous, but I'm working with several doctors on a stem cell project to help with bone regrowth and rejuvenation. I got this idea when I watched the healing process after Graciela's first two surgeries. She didn't get the results her surgeon and I wanted and we felt that if the bone growth cycle could be altered, that she could get a better outcome. My goal is still to get her walking again and out of her wheelchair.

She uses that thing like armor to keep people away. She's beautiful, funny and smart and I don't want her to feel held back any longer."

"Stem cell research?! Where? How?" Ellie asked, flabbergasted with his response.

"Well, it all came about at first one day when I was cleaning the bio lab in the physician's assistant program. They share the lab with the students in the premed two-year program and the professor and I started talking. He's very over-qualified for his job at a junior college but retired from a more demanding job at a health research job at the CDC. He said he wanted less stress in his life. He was excited by the ideas I was talking about, and we decided to work on a project in his lab after hours when we were off work and there were no classes scheduled into the lab. He had contacts at Johns Hopkins, Cornell and the Mayo Clinic. He had read some journals that hinted at the concepts I'd come up with and wanted us to form a partnership and collaborate with these other schools to investigate my theories which happened to align with theirs. I know this sounds impossible, like a fairy tale or a *telenovela* (TV soap opera), but it's all true. I feel very fortunate to have met Eric Stockman when I did."

"It is rather unbelievable, Noé. Even you have to agree with that. It just means how important it is for you to improve your English so you can pass the medical board tests here and get your American credentials. It seems even more ridiculous that you have to work as a custodian during the day when you should be free to work on your research,"

"Once again, you're right, *mi amor*. We have to make time to do that if you don't mind. When I see you, I forget to think about things like English and research. I came over here with no plan to even do more than kiss you hello and good-bye and I'm here on the couch with you, wanting to kiss like we're in high school, trying to find a few hidden moments. I don't want you to think this is all about sex, Ellie. You are too important to me," Noé said as held her face in his hands, memorizing her features.

Unable to resist, Ellie leaned in for a kiss. "Would it make you feel better if I told you that you make me crazy? I feel like some sex-starved teenager who can't wait to get you along for some more stolen, hidden moments. Sex is definitely part of this, Noé; I can't deny it, but there's more. I don't know what that is yet, but I feel there's more."

"I agree. Now, can we watch TV, so we're occupied with something other than wrapping our arms around each other and kissing? I am trying to be noble here and do what's right on our only second date," Noé said wryly.

"Second date. Yes, it is, but we made love on our first. How's that for doing things backwards? I don't even know what to say at this point. Here' let's watch a movie," Ellie said and got up to get the channel changer and turned to a movie channel. Back in her seat, she snuggled comfortably under Noé's arm, and they did watch that movie after all.

Chapter 6: Drama at School

Things were going well in the Adult Ed classes during the next week, and students and staff were settling into their routines of group work, teacher tutoring and computer time. Everyone was busy when Ellie heard some loud voices from the room next door, Courtney's room.

"Excuse me, class. I need to check on what's happening next door," and Ellie hurried to the connecting door. She quickly took in the scene. Courtney was standing near the door between the aggressive sounding man who was at her door yelling at her and at some of the students.

Ellie went up to him and asked him in Spanish if she could help him with something because the curses and comments he was yelling were in Spanish. An errant thought ran through her mind that he was at least cursing in Mexican Spanish, and she could match him with curses though she doubted that would be the best professional approach.

"*¡Me robaron mis carnales! Tenemos cosas que hacer, güey. Estas pinches clases les están chingando con tus mentes? Vénganse conmigo. Ahorita,*" (You stole my brothers. We have things to do, dude. These damn classes are fucking with your minds. Come with me. Right now.) he shouted at them.

"Excuse me, but I'm Ellie Thompson, and what's your name?" Ellie said as she stepped in front of Courtney and pushed her back a little.

He seemed taken aback by her request and stopped his tirade, but only for a moment. "*Vete de aquí, bolilla. No te metas en cosas que no son tuyas!* (Get out of here, white girl/honkey. Don't put your nose in things that aren't any of your business.)

Ellie saw him glance over her shoulder, and she wondered what he saw because he did stop shouting for the moment. Then quickly Harry, one of her GED guys, ran up to the door with Davis Jenkins and Noé right behind. Ellie started to worry for her students and everyone in the class because her GED men were now inside the room near the connecting door looking threatening.

"Oye, vale más que te vayas sin causar más problemas aquí. (Listen, it's better that you go without causing more problems here.) *Vámonos.* (Let's go.) Noé said as he approached the intruder with his hands open and extended.

Ellie was watching it all like it was in slow motion. She could see Courtney's tears silently rolling down her cheek and her trembling slightly but looking the intruder in the eye. She could see her GED men there to help protect too and she was really glad that Davis and Noé had shown up and that Harry had shown the foresight to go for help.

There was a collective gasp when the intruder pulled a knife and started to advance towards the teachers. Noé didn't hesitate and he kicked the knife out of the man's hands and then kicked him in the knees to take him down. Immediately, Noé and Davis were on top of him then, holding him down as he struggled violently.

"¡Cállese el hocico! Ahora te va a salir mal, muy mal. Pasaste de límite, cabrón. Esto no se hace aquí en la escuela. ¡Qué

vergüenza ser mexicano como tú y ver esto pasar!" (Shut your trap! Now it's going to end badly, very badly for you. You passed the limit, asshole. This isn't done here in the school. What shame to be Mexican like you and see this happen!) Noé spoke to him with deadly calm and a threatening look on his face. His jaw was clenched tightly and he looked furious.

Just then, the campus security came running to the doorway and sirens could be heard in the background. The sheriff and the Wharton police departments also descended on the campus in quick response. The sheriff quickly handcuffed the man and picked up the knife as they hauled him out of the room.

"I can see we have plenty of witnesses. I'll need to take your statements now from everyone who saw what happened. Is there a room close by we can interview people?"

Then Dave Morris came running along with the college president. Both appeared winded, and their faces were red and sweaty. Hearing the request, the security guard got on his radio and then said, "Right across the hall. I can open several rooms for you right now."

After the law enforcement had left, Ellie gathered all the students and teachers in her room to talk to them about what had happened.

"I appreciate all everyone did to try to help with our unwelcome intruder earlier. Miss Courtney showed courage and common sense in her positioning of herself to keep him at the door. Harry, going for Mr. Jenkins and Mr. Vásquez was outstanding decision making. My GED men, thank you for your presence at the door to have my back. I'm glad that none of our students tried to get more involved because I think that would have set him off more and you could have been hurt. To the Hispanic men who knew this guy, good work in keeping calm and not getting into a shouting match with him. Ignoring his words was the best choice and I'm sure it wasn't easy.

I have to say that in all my years of teaching, especially teaching adults, I've never seen anything like this. If he weren't going to jail, I'd say that our intruder needs some more education, but I'd rather it was somewhere else. They do have GED classes in prison. But, he's not important to us. He was trying to get his guys to come with him, trying to convince them they didn't want to better themselves. That's not the kind of friend anyone needs. I'm glad no one was hurt and thanks to you all for your keeping calm through all that drama. You all impressed me, and I appreciate each of you for what you did and did not do today."

"Miss Ellie, how about Mr. Vásquez? He's got some skills. Right? That's a badass boyfriend you've got." Leroy said as he and his friends nodded their heads.

Blushing, Ellie just looked at him shaking her head and then said, "If it's OK with everyone, I think we should dismiss early today. I will talk to the campus president and head of security about their starting new procedures to keep people like our intruder off this campus. One thing we will do is keep our doors locked at all times to start. Your safety is very important to me. So, no more jokes about me and out you go," Ellie said laughing.

The four Hispanic students approached her and apologized for their friend's behavior. Ellie and Courtney assured them it wasn't their fault. They should be proud that they're here trying to better themselves and not to let their former friend bring them down.

Once the last of the students left, Ellie sat down with Courtney and Trace, "Courtney, you were tremendous today. I know you were afraid; I was afraid also and all of the rest of us were. I'm serious about being impressed with your judgement under extreme pressure. Not everybody could have handled today's drama as well as you did. Let me reassure you that this isn't an everyday occurrence in education, especially in adult education. Typically, this kind of stunt happens in high school or middle school. You've seen all that's on social media and TV about why people do these things. I'll bet our gang banger guy from today didn't post a manifesto on Facebook though. He was an aberration, afraid he was being left behind by his friends, which is true. I think your new Hispanic group of men will be very devoted learners if they weren't already. I was impressed with their math scores from the placement test. I'll just be doing a little review with them as they're already on high school level. I think you'll find they'll progress rapidly," Ellie said and smiled at Courtney who still looked a little pale and shell-shocked.

"Oh, and Trace, I saw that you kept your students in your room and closed the connecting door. Good thinking on your part too. I want to stress that this is not a usual day for a teacher at any level. I'm glad you both are so cool under extreme stress. Each of you did exactly the right thing not to escalate the situation. Sometimes, it takes doing very little to calm things down. I've never seen things improve when people started all yelling at each other. Like I said to our students, 'Go home'."

After locking up, Ellie went to find Davis Jenkins in his office but found it empty and followed the voices to their break room.

"You shoulda seen Vásquez here do some karate shit and kick the knife outta the S.O.B.'s hand and then kick him in the knees to bring him down," Davis said enthusiastically.

"Well, I couldn't have kept him down if you hadn't jumped in then to help. Together we kept him there till the police could come and handcuff him. I'm just glad that Harry came to find you and I was there to be able to go help with you."

Ellie walked in and singled out the two men and said, "I want to thank you both for coming to rescue us today. I hate to think what would have happened if both of you hadn't shown up when you did. Harry made an excellent choice to quietly leave my room and go find you guys. Thanks again!" Ellie said with heartfelt emotion.

"Well, Miss Ellie, I'm glad that my nephew Harry came for us, for sure. I'm also glad that my lead custodian knows karate and he was with me when Harry came. I can't say that I knew about all that, but I'm glad it turned out well. Did you notice, Miss Ellie, that your GED crew had your back too? They were all there ready to jump in."

"Oh, Mr. Jenkins, I'm glad they didn't though I did appreciate the show of force that they presented to our intruder. I think they played a role in containing the situation though if the two of you hadn't arrived when you did, I'm afraid someone would have gotten hurt. "I'm going over now to meet with the president and head of security about what measures we have in place now and what we need to add to keep us all safe. I think you should be part of the discussion too, Mr. Davis, because if things need to be modified or added to, you will have the knowledge to say what can be done right away and what would need more time. Will you come with me? I'll call ahead to tell them I'm bringing you," Ellie said earnestly.

"Don't you mean you're asking if you can bring the head custodian to the meeting?" Davis said wryly.

"No, I'm telling them. I know how campuses run, Mr. Jenkins, and the custodial staff understand the buildings and grounds better than any of the folks in their administrative offices. If they don't know that, then they should, and they'll learn that today. You're an important resource here on this campus. You are a behind-the-scenes reason things run so well. Don't you agree?"

"Yes, I do. I'll be there as long as you call ahead so they're not caught off guard. You might want to give them a few reasons to want me at that meeting. It wouldn't hurt," Davis said and looked at Ellie expectantly.

"I'm on that now. Just give me a minute," Ellie said as she smiled at both the men, at the room in general and turned to go, dialing the number.

Ellie could hear in the background the comments coming from the room while she waited to be transferred to the president. "So that's your woman, Vásquez? No wonder you hauled your ass over there so fast. She's fine looking. What? I'm only saying what everyone's thinking," Tom said chuckling.

"Mr. Whitehall, this is Ellie Thompson, and I just wanted to talk to you about someone I'm bringing to the meeting with me, Davis Jenkins. He's the head custodian here and knows more about the buildings, grounds and systems in place than anyone. He'll be able to help us better assess what we currently have in place and how fast we can implement some changes. We'll be over soon. Alright? Yes. Thank you, Ted."

"Mr. Jenkins, consider yourself invited to the meeting. Now will you come with me?"

"Yes, ma'am. That's all I needed to hear. Let's get going. Noé, you're in charge if anything comes up. Hopefully, you won't need karate to take care of it," Davis said laughing as he got up to accompany Ellie to the campus president's office.

After an hour-long meeting between the college president, the head of Human Resources, the head of security, Ellie and Davis Jenkins, they broke up with plans to meet again next week for a progress check. Ellie came away with specifics she could tell her teachers and students that would be in place starting tomorrow as well as information on existing and planned security cameras and the patrols of the security team that were going to be increased as soon as they could hire another two men with local law enforcement filling in till then.

President Whitehall commented to Ellie that he was glad she'd shown the initiative to bring along the head custodian because he'd had many insightful and useful comments to contribute to the meeting.

"It only made good sense to me. When I worked as an associate principal at a large Sugar Land high school, the head custodians worked with me often on many projects to keep the school functioning. They knew all the ins and outs of the various systems, storage, high traffic areas with blind spots for our cameras and just about everything else. They were a valued resource. From what I've seen of Mr. Jenkins and his staff, I knew it would be the same here. Thanks for including him."

"Anyways, well done."

Walking back to their area, Davis and Ellie were recapping the meeting and sharing their comments on the outcome. They agreed that they'd addressed the immediate needs and were glad that monies would be found to install more security cameras and beef up the monitoring system with more receivers as well as hiring more security personnel and instituting a partnership with local law enforcement to help patrol the campus as it was spread out over twenty acres.

"Well, I am glad to see this day come to an end. I imagine your boyfriend's heart has stopped racing by now. I have to admit that when we got to your room it was worse actually seeing that guy than imagining what was happening based on Harry's details. The knife was a new detail that scared us all, I think. All of us had an adrenaline rush about then," Davis and took his hat off to give it a shake and then placed it over his bald head.

"Davis, did you used to be an athlete in your younger days? If you don't mind my asking."

"Why would you ask that, Ellie? That's a strange question."

"Not strange after you ran from your office to my room hardly breaking a sweat and then you proceeded to sit on that man with no effort to keep him pinned. Also, it was no stranger than seeing Noé turn into a karate master at just the right moment. It seems that there's a lot I don't know about people around here though I'm glad both of you had those skills when we needed them."

"Ah, yes, Noé was a surprise, but he always is, isn't he? Did he tell you about his lab work with one of our bio profs here? Not exactly what I expected from one of my custodians. In fact, that's never happened to me before with my custodial staff, so seeing him doing those karate kicks didn't surprise me all that much. He's always full of surprises," Davis said with a laugh.

"Good point. Yes, he did tell me about his experiment in the bio lab. I guess we're all good for a surprise or two, but his seem to be of the extreme variety," Ellie said laughing and smiling as she looked ahead and saw Noé standing outside her building and waiting for her.

"I think we're all off the clock now. I'll see you tomorrow and hope that my teachers are brave enough to come back. They're brand new and so young. I can see where today may give them nightmares. We shall see. Thank you again for helping us out today. It could have ended so differently. Bye now," Ellie said and saluted Davis as they neared her building and took different paths on the sidewalk.

"Noé, I'm so happy to see you!" Ellie said as he crushed her in a hug, lifted her up and swung her around.

"*Mi amor.* I shouldn't even hug you here for the world to see, but I was so worried today when I came into the classroom and saw that lunatic with a knife threatening you. Can we go somewhere together tonight? I really need to talk through this and need some time with you to realize you are OK. My mind keeps going to 'What if?' again and again."

Unwrapping herself from Noé's tight hug, Ellie said, "I'd love to see you tonight. First, I have to go home to check on Flo and Duke, my dog, and then I'm yours."

"Would you like to go out to eat, or can I cook something for you tonight? I know my kitchen looks like a gourmet cook resides there and I'm not, but I can grill a steak, put together a salad and microwave some potatoes. You tell me what you'd prefer," Noé said seriously with a slight smile. It was evident he was still shaken by what had happened today in the classroom.

"Your house it is then. It'll be more relaxing than sitting at a restaurant. I'd like to talk about today also and I don't think I want to do that out in public. I don't want people talking about this other than the statement the president gives to the news and local paper. I'm afraid someone might overhear any conversation we would have about the incident," Ellie said and then felt like a weight had lifted. She hadn't realized that she needed that closure with Noé till just now when they arranged the date for this evening.

Chapter 7: Dinner at Noé's

Ellie went home, showered, changed her outfit from work clothes to casual, fed Duke and briefly explained to Flo what had happened at work that day. She felt she had to in case it made the evening news because Flo would have called her immediately for the details and to be sure Ellie was OK even though she'd already seen her. It took some convincing, but finally Flo admitted that Ellie did look fine and seemed no worse for having gone through the incident. When she explained she was going over to Noé's for dinner, Flo got a smug look.

"Alright, what's the look for, Auntie Flo?"

"I can bet he's going to go all cave man on you. Be prepared for a wild night. You may think you're going for dinner, but sex is life-affirming, and I imagine it freaked him out to see you in danger today. Did you put on nice undies?"

"Flo! And, yes, I did. Bye now," Ellie said as she walked by and gave Flo a kiss on the cheek, laughing as she went out the door.

Using her GPS, Ellie managed to find her way back to Noe's. Since it was still daylight, she could appreciate the trees and the design of his very modern and huge house. His yard was like a park with so many towering pecan trees. Interspersed were many live oak trees as well. The lawn was cut and was a perfect backdrop to the big house with its modern lines, metal roof and many darkened windows. Another odd thing that didn't seem as odd now for him to own this luxurious house that she knew he'd been an orthopedic surgeon in Mexico City. While his custodian's job here couldn't afford this house, his salary as a surgeon in Mexico certainly could.

Knocking on the door, Ellie heard a deep woof. Noé appeared at the door and when he opened it, a huge fawn mastiff ran out and sniffed her legs where Duke had rubbed against her before she left her home a little while ago.

"Lola, véngase para acá. (Come here.) Excuse her pushiness, Ellie. She seems to smell your dog on your legs and shorts. Come in and I'll put her up," Noé said as he grabbed Lola's collar and pulled her back in beside him.

Ellie walked by and stopped to give him a brief kiss and went towards the kitchen. "I didn't see her last time I was here. Is she a new addition?"

"Lola? No. She's been with me for almost ten years. I got her when Graciela was recovering from one of her surgeries though Lola's such an oaf, I guess she wasn't the best choice. Graci loves her though which was the main idea even if not so practical. Last time you were here, she was at the vet's for her annual checkup and they had to sedate her to clean her teeth as well as give her a spa day, so she spent the night. Oh, watch for the slobber," Noé said as Lola shook her head.

"I forgot you haven't met Duke yet. He was in the back yard and then my oldest daughter Rachel stopped by before you came over and took him for a sleepover at her house, saying she missed him too much. He's a Saint Bernard about Lola's size and is also a drooler. So, no worries in that regard. I'm glad you like big dogs too."

"To me, they're the real dogs. They don't whine or have that high, annoying bark. Little dogs are so unpredictable and grumpy too, whereas big dogs like ours are pretty laid back."

"Exactly. I'm glad you understand. I have to say that the few times I tried dating after Chad, they were all afraid of my dog and couldn't get past his size and drooling. He didn't like any of them. I guess he did a little bit of growling in a rumbling sort of way," Ellie admitted reluctantly.

"I see Duke's a good judge of character. We'll have to introduce him to Lola, and they can have a play date. What do you think?" Noé asked hopefully.

"Perfect idea. I rarely go to dog parks because he's too big to play with the little dogs without hurting them accidentally. He'd like playing with someone his size I think."

"Are you hungry? If you are, let's go to the kitchen and get dinner started. It won't take long at all to get things ready. Would you help me make the salad?" Noé said as he took Ellie's hand and headed to the back of the house to the kitchen.

"You weren't kidding about a gourmet kitchen. That gas range looks industrial size, and I see it has a grill in the middle. Let's get started on that salad while you heat up the grill and start the potatoes. OK?"

Ellie heard the steaks start to sizzle and then she felt Noé come up behind her and then put his hands on top of hers while she was chopping the lettuce and tomatoes. He then wrapped his arms loosely around her waist and kissed her once softly on her neck and then again."

"Noé, I have a sharp knife in my hand, and I'd hate to lose a finger because I'm too distracted to concentrate," Ellie admonished while she leaned back into Noé's' muscular body and tilted her head to give him better access to her neck.

"Well, then *mi amor,* put the damn knife down. I'm on a mission here."

"Oh, is that right?" Ellie teased and turned around and put her arms around his neck, pulling him closer and kissed his mouth and then his cheek and down to his neck. Two can play at that game, sir."

"Ellie I'm too old to be clever with my words but know, please, that I want you right now but first I have to feed you. We have some work to do before we can relax, I'm afraid. There are some ghosts to banish before we can really enjoy the night and ourselves. Agreed?"

They sat down to dinner a short while later and Noé was right when he said he could grill a good steak. Ellie ate till she was full and then pushed her chair back a little from the table. "Noé, that was delicious. I definitely feel more relaxed and satisfied after a delicious meal. Thank you. You can cook for me any time you want."

"You are welcome, Ellie. It was my pleasure to feed you dinner tonight. I really wanted, no needed, to spend some time with you to eliminate the bad memories from this afternoon at work. I am so glad that you weren't hurt. Come, let's get a cup of decaf and go sit in the family room so we can talk a little. OK?"

"Yes, of course. Let's get the coffee and go."

Noé led her to a large, high-ceilinged room to the right of the kitchen and dining area. There were heavy wooden beams drawing the eye up. The room looked huge. He led her to a big, leather sectional that faced the ceiling-high rock fireplace.

"Come, sit with me here and let's talk."

"Noé, I'd like to start by thanking you for saving me and my students and teacher today. If you hadn't come in and overpowered that guy, any one of us could have been hurt. It was such a relief to see you, and I have to say amazing to watch you in action. I had no idea. You're just one surprise after another, Mr. Vásquez."

"Ah, *tesoro* (treasure/baby), you have no idea what I felt when I walked in and saw that asshole. My heart almost stopped. It was bad enough I could hear him shouting at you in the hall running to your room, but when I saw the knife, I didn't think; I just reacted. I'm glad I had all those years of karate growing up and then Graciela and I used to take classes together at the same dojo before her accident."

"Why doesn't that surprise me, Noé? I don't think there's anything you've ever wanted to learn that you haven't become a master of. I mean, who leaves a career as an engineer to go back to school to become a doctor and then goes on to become a surgeon? You do realize that most people don't achieve all these things, don't you?"

"Ah, Ellie, really, it's nothing. I'm just glad I had the skills and could be there to protect you. I don't know what I would do if something happened to you. It's all so new, but already you're too important to me. I'm sorry if this is too intense. I can even hear myself sounding like some crazed fanatic, so forgive me my feelings. Today was horrible!"

"Noé, we seem to do most things backwards. I mean we slept together on the first date and now we're trying to get to

know each other. My feelings are intense
too, but maybe tonight is just a reaction to
today's scary, near-death situation. I have to
tell you that my Aunt Flo said you might
feel like this; that it was a common reaction
to danger."

"She did? What else did she say?"

"She asked me if I was wearing sexy
underwear."

"I'm beginning to really like your Aunt
Flo. Well, are you?"

"Am I what? Oh, you mean am I wearing
sexy underwear? Wanna see?" Ellie said
with a chuckle.

"Wait, *mi amor*. Would you like to go to
my bedroom this time instead of making
love on one of my couches? While I think
my couches are comfortable, I think it would
even be nicer on a bed, my big, comfortable
bed. What do you think?" Noé said as he
stood and pulled Ellie up.

"If I knew where it was, I'd race you to
that bed, Noé. Show me the way."

"This way, *mi reina*, (my queen)"

"Noe, have I told you yet that I love your
house? It's really nice and your yard is like a
park," Ellie said and gestured around in the
spacious bedroom that had a wall of
windows with some kind of tint to keep out
the sun.

"Thanks. You know I bought it sight unseen. I knew I wanted to come to Wharton and just looked online. It had the wooden floors and wide-open spaces I wanted for Graciela to be able to easily get around in her wheelchair. Also, there are thirteen acres of land around the house with all these trees and some pasture too though I can't imagine getting horses again any time soon. Another positive factor was I'm close to a college both South in Victoria and North in Sugar Land though I'll probably have to go into Houston if I ever get to the stage of doing another residency.

"Won't Graciela live in Austin while she's going to school?"

"Yes, but I hope she'll come home to visit often. At least that's my plan though it might not be hers. I guess I'll have to wait and see. She should be coming here soon either way."

"I think we've done enough house touring tonight, if that's OK with you?" Noé said as he wrapped his arms around Ellie and pulled her toward the bed. "I've been waiting all through dinner and coffee to see that sexy underwear you told Flo about."

Ellie chuckled and giggled when Noé kissed her neck where it met her shoulder.

"Tickles."

Soon there was a pile of clothes on the chair near the window as Noé kept tossing his and Ellie's clothes one by one over there. He carefully laid her back on the bed and then moved down her body a little to suckle her breasts. Ellie moaned her approval though she doubted he needed any. He already seemed to know what pleased her and drove her wild. *'I do love a fast learner in bed with me! Chad never got it right in five years and this man already has me melting and we've just started this relationship.'*

After sucking on both her breasts, he gave them a final kiss and moved down to kiss her belly button. Holding her breath in anticipation, Ellie waited for him to make his way lower. She knew what he was going to do next and couldn't wait to experience the sensation of him sucking on her clit again. *'This man knows what to do with his mouth. My lady parts are on high alert here.'*

Noé didn't disappoint and he was soon licking and sucking on her clit while Ellie writhed in ecstasy on the bed, her fingers gripping the satiny, soft sheets. He put two fingers inside her and fucked her with his hand while he used his tongue on her clit to drive her to an orgasm. Shuddering with release, Ellie watched him, eyes half open while Noé tore open a condom and rolled it on his erection.

'Even watching him do that makes me hot. Hotter. What he does to my body is something I've waited for, forever really. It was never like this with Chad or anyone else.'

As he slowly pushed inside her wet pussy, Noé held her hips in place, eyes closed as he enjoyed every part of their joining. Soon, he was fully inside, his balls resting against her body. Opening his eyes to find hers, Noé began to thrust, Ellie meeting him each time by raising her hips to meet him. Before long, they were thrusting in a steady rhythm that brought them both to orgasm. After a moment, Noé withdrew and when he went to remove the condom, said, "Ellie, the condom tore. *Híjole. ¡Chingado!*(Wow. Fuck!) We have a problem, *querida.(*love)"

"Oh, Noé, don't worry. I wish we had a problem. Remember what I said Chad told me about our tests that my womb is not a good environment to conceive or carry a baby?

"Ah, mi amor. What if that's changed? That was at least a dozen years ago. Yes?"

"Yes, it was. But the tests said it was impossible and that wouldn't change. So, don't worry. It'll be fine," Ellie reassured him.

"Just suppose you could get pregnant and did? What would you want to do?"

"Do? I've wanted to carry a baby in my womb my whole life, Noé. I don't know what you'd do, but I'd carry and keep a baby. Even if you don't want one," Ellie said, clearly annoyed and clear in her voice.

"Wait. Wait a minute. While this isn't something I was even remotely planning or thinking about, I would never do anything to end a pregnancy, Ellie. I want you to know that. We keep saying we're moving fast here in our relationship though this might be supersonic speed to conceive a baby at this stage."

"I'm glad we agree on having a baby then rather than aborting one because I do believe it's a woman's choice, but that's not my choice. We'll just have to see what happens. OK?"

"Agreed. Do you know how long we'll have to wait to be sure, Ellie? I guess I'm asking where you are in your cycle, *mi amor*."

"Well, this is certainly an unusual second date conversation, Mr. Vásquez. Shows that you're a doctor, I guess. I'm actually right in the middle, which should be the most fertile time if I were only fertile. I've felt like a useless woman ever since Chad and I tried so hard to conceive a baby. All those shots made my hormones go crazy and I felt like I was on an emotional roller coaster. So much time and money went into that never-ending journey of failure. I'm glad that's not the discussion though this has to be the oddest date conversation I've ever had."

Ignoring the rest of Ellie's comments, Noé focused on her cycle. "Well, we shall see, won't we? Should be an interesting two weeks for us. Let's just wait and see what will be. Right now, I'd like to just stay here in bed with you and lie close together. Come here, *mi amor*. Let me hold you."

'If I'd created this man from my imagination, I wouldn't change a thing. I must be dreaming about some romance novel I just read and loved. He always says and does the right thing. He's so caring and tender and incredible in bed. In my years of marriage, I never felt so loved and taken care of as I do in this man's arms. If we by some miracle get pregnant, I'm glad it was with Noé. I'm afraid to let myself hope again that it could be possible.'

After a while, Ellie awoke when a cold nose touched her cheek and was then followed by a big dog's kiss. Laughing, Ellie turned to Noé and kissed him on the cheek. "I think Lola wants something. Does she need to go out?"

"Not really. She has a doggie door in the utility room to go out whenever she wants. She just wants some attention, I guess. Again, I'm glad you're a dog person too. Not everybody understands a cold nose wake up call."

"Ellie, it's late. I think you should go back home, or Aunt Flo will worry. I'd rather you spent the night in my bed, but she will want to question you in the morning about if your sexy underwear got looked at and had any effect on me. You must be sure to tell her that they were sexy and were quite a motivator. I don't know if I'd tell her we're on pregnancy watch though. But whatever you think is fine with me."

"You're too funny. You and Auntie Flo think too much alike. And I don't think I'll tell her about our pregnancy watch yet. She'd be so excited if I got pregnant because she knows how hard I tried and how much I wanted it all those years ago."

Ellie got up reluctantly and put on her sexy underwear, her clothes and looked for her shoes.

"Family room. We left our shoes in the family room."

"Next you're going to tell me you're psychic. Yes, I do remember that now," Ellie said with a laugh as she moved toward the door.

Noé was quickly at her side and held her hand as they walked through the hallway toward the family room with Lola walking along beside them. Reaching the family room, Ellie and Noé put on their shoes and then Ellie got her purse to go outside. Noé opened the door for her, and he and Lola walked Ellie to her car. When she reached her car, they turned to each other and embraced. Noé rested his forehead against Ellie's, no longer feeling the anxiety he had earlier seeing her confronted with a knife-wielding man. The evening had had a perfect ending, and he wasn't going to worry about what-ifs about a pregnancy. *Lo qué mande Dios.* (Whatever God wills.)

Kissing her one last time, Noe said, "Goodnight, *querida*. Please text me when you get home. I'll see you tomorrow at work. Yes?"

"Yes. I'm looking forward to a calm, quiet, uneventful day. Thank you for tonight, Noé. For the way you treat me and what you said tonight. Your words mean so much to me," Ellie said quietly and then opened the door and got into her car.

Getting home about ten minutes later, Ellie opened the door to find Flo sitting in the living room with Rachel and Wendy, all watching a movie.

"Girls! What a nice surprise!" Ellie said, smiling hugely to see her two oldest children.

"Ah, mom. We had to check up on you. Auntie Flo said you had a hot date tonight, so we came over to get the news about your new guy," Rachel said, speaking for both of them as she usually did.

"Geez. Word travels fast around here. Yes, I did have a date with my new guy. The guy who saved my life today as I'm sure your Auntie Flo has already told you. He fixed me a wonderful dinner tonight and we talked about everything that went down today."

"Aw. Auntie Flo said you wore sexy underwear. Is that it? Surely there's more to your evening." Wendy asked, looking at Flo for confirmation.

"Again, with my underwear. I don't even know what to say to that, but I will tell you that I was glad I wore them. And that's all I'm going to say on that topic."

"Well done, Ellie! It's about time," Flo started and finished with the girls joining in.

"Ok, enough, you three. Have I told you lately how lucky I am to still have you in my life after all these years? You guys make me so happy and proud," Ellie said as she went over to her girls to give them each a hug.

"Back at you Mom. I'm glad we were there for you during those years when you wanted a baby so much. I know teens and preteens aren't like a sweet little baby, but we tried," Wendy said.

"Oh, so am I. Those were such hard years for me. The four of you kept me going. While I was going through hard times emotionally, you guys made me so proud and happy each day. I couldn't have made it through those years without you guys."

"What I never understood was why Dad put you through all of that," Rachel said frowning.

"What do you mean, daughter? What do you mean your Dad put me through all of that? It was a process we had to go through to try to conceive a baby unfortunately."

"Oh, man. Our Dad is more of a shit than I thought. Mom, he had an operation last year because his current girlfriend he's engaged to wants a baby. He had his vasectomy reversed a few weeks ago. He told us last year that he had the vasectomy done right after Mike was born. Our bio mom didn't want any more kids and he didn't either. That was the first we heard about it."

"What?! Vasectomy?! If he were right in front of me, I swear I'd choke him to death. That explains why he was always the one to read me the test results, to explain all the technical things the doctor had to say. He probably paid him off to not tip me off. I went through hell with all those shots that messed up my hormones and emotions and then the sorrow and sense of failure each month were more than depressing. I can't believe he could be so cruel. I hope I never see that piece of shit again. Sorry to talk about your father that way, girls," Ellie said, choking off sobs as she realized what an awful game her ex-husband had played with her and her feelings.

Flo, Rachel and Wendy all got up to go give Ellie a hug, hardly able to believe the cruelty of Chad. It was a monstrous thing that he had done. He had stolen those years of fertility from her in the most callous way, causing her so many emotional upheavals. "Shit, this should be a TV show or on Jerry Springer or Maury Povich. Normal people don't pull shit like this. I was so stupid. I should have demanded that Chad show me all the paperwork from our testing. I was just so upset when he told me the news that I couldn't get past that. I was crying too much to make sense of anything I'd have tried to read anyway. I'm glad to finally know the truth though. I hope it doesn't upset you to hear me talk about your father this way, but honestly, I can't seem to help it and shut my mouth about his treachery. This goes beyond bullying. It was cruel, incredibly cruel."

"Don't feel you have to hold back, Mom. It's even worse than we knew. We will have to tell Trey and Mike about this. They deserve to know what a creep their father is. You know you can count on us. We're your kids and always will be. You're the only mom we ever had. We had nannies and a stint or two at boarding school before you married Chad," Wendy said, her eyes filling with tears also.

"Tell us something good, Mom. How about your new boyfriend? That sounds like a much better topic. Auntie Flo told us about your day plus we watched it on the news. I thought this was a quiet, little rural town. Stuff like what happened to you today sounds like a big city or suburban problem, not a small town like this," Rachel said, wiping her eyes and making an effort to change their focus onto something very different from their dad Chad.

"Well, my new boyfriend is Noé and he's a custodian at the junior college in town where I've started working. He's a custodian that seems to be second in command of the department. But he's a doctor, a surgeon from Mexico, who's here to learn English. He has to take medical board exams in English here. He moved here because his daughter Graciela is coming to Texas to get her master's at UT Austin. He lives in a mega house here in town. I didn't know he knew karate too. He's also a certified civil engineer."

"This man sounds like a superhero. Is there anything he can't do? His story is almost unbelievable. Are you sure?" Wendy asked, concerned her mom was being deceived again.

"Yes, I am sure. I've seen his diplomas and licenses on the wall at his house, and I watched him use karate to kick the knife out of our intruder's hand not three feet away. Then he took the guy down to the ground, also right in front of me. I haven't met his daughter yet, but I think I will soon. He does sound too good to be true, but the wonderful part is it's all true. I feel like I've known him forever and we get along so well."

"Auntie, Flo. What's your take on this new man in Mom's life? Do you approve? I guess we need to give him some credit for saving her life today as well as her students. Right?" Rachel asked, smiling at Ellie.

"Well, there is that matter of his superhero actions today. Before then, he'd already won me over. He's such a gentleman, so polite and caring. He has my approval though it doesn't seem like our Ellie is waiting for approval from any of us. Did you get that statement she made about underwear earlier? Flo smirked and said with a wry smile.

"I think we're going to have to keep more in touch with Mom. Now that she's back in Texas, it's easy for us to keep tabs on her. It's going to be fun to watch her dating. That's something we've never experienced with her though we watched Chad with his parade of bimbos in and out the door for years. That was just annoying, but we're going to enjoy this," Wendy said, very happy with the turn of events for their mom who looked happier than they'd seen her look for years.

"I agree but have to say first that anyone who can put a smile on her face like she has now is doing something right. I can't wait to meet the new man," Rachel said and looked expectantly at Ellie.

"Alright, everyone calm down. Maybe we can have a big get-together when Noé's daughter comes to town, and we can all meet each other. I'll keep you posted. And thanks, girls. I love seeing you and love having your support along with Auntie Flo. I'm a lucky woman. I have the best kids and aunt in my corner. I've been so happy being your mom, girls. I hope you know that."

"As if we couldn't. You tell us all the time how much you love us individually and as a group and how proud you are of all of us. No doubts here," Rachel joked and then ended seriously, emotion evident in the look she gave Ellie.

"Ditto, Mom," Wendy seconded.

Chapter 8: Back to School

The next day, Ellie walked into her office a little apprehensively, not even sure her rookie teachers would be back after the last day they'd had. She could understand if they chose to quit though she didn't know what she'd do to cover their classes if they did. It would all work itself out in the next half hour one way or another. *Patience.*

Knocking on her door, Noé stuck his head in to say, "Good morning, *querida.* Ready for the new day to begin soon? I have to say that it's going to be anti-climactic after everything that happened yesterday. Any worries? Is there anything I can do?"

"Hi, Noé, Good morning to you. I have to agree that today is going to seem dull compared to yesterday's drama and danger, but I can deal with that. That's for sure. I'm looking forward to a boring day and less adrenalin flowing. At the moment my only worry is if my young teachers will be brave enough to return to work today. I'm sure they were scared shitless yesterday on their first day of real teaching ever. Poor things. We'll see. And, no, there's nothing you can do, but I do appreciate your coming by to see how I was doing. You take good care of me," Ellie said and blushed.

"That is my pleasure, *mi amor.* If the head of security doesn't show up soon with a radio for you, I'll bring you one of ours. Just call me if you still need one. Use channel two if you need anything. Having been an assistant principal, you know how to use one. It's the same model commonly used in schools around here. I'll check on that right now. See you later, Ellie," Noé left, and she could hear him talking on the radio to reach the security guy.

Ellie could hear voices in the hall then as the head of security, Norvell Jones, came down her hallway, talking to Noé on his radio. In seconds, he was inside her office and handing her a radio. "They told me you were an AP before, so you'll know how to use this. Channel 2 is what we're all on, so call for help if you need it. Questions?"

"No, Mr. Jones. I appreciate your giving me this. It'll make us all feel safer knowing we can communicate with you and ask for help immediately though I sure hope nothing like yesterday's fiasco happens again. Thank you for your help yesterday ending the incident and also for your thoughts during the meeting with the president. Your insights about campus security helped us put together a good plan, I think."

"You're welcome, Ms. Thompson. I want to tell you that things like that don't happen here. I've been here five years and nothing like that has happened and the man I replaced was here seven years and never had an incident to deal with either. We'll all be more careful and watchful now though. You have a good day, now ma'am," Norvell said, nodding his head to Ellie, turned and left.

Holding the radio in her hand brought back memories of when she was an assistant principal in high school. The radios were the lifeline that kept all the administrators, their secretaries, the head custodian and the campus police officer in contact throughout the school day. They were essential in controlling problems to keep them from escalating and calling for help when needed. *'I hadn't thought about my life as a high school assistant principal in a while. There were lots of ups and downs with that job. So much pressure. At least I don't feel that pressure here.'*

Just then, Trey and Courtney walked into her office though neither one looked sure about their being back at the college.

"Hello! Glad to see you today bright and early. I won't pretend that yesterday must have made you question yourselves and your reasons for taking this job here. A job is a job though and sometimes we need one even if we're not sure we want it. I'm really pleased you're here. Let's get to our rooms.

"Remember to lock your doors and look out the window before you let anyone in. We're fortunate that this building already has windows in the doors so we can see who's outside without the window posing a risk that someone could break it and reach in to unlock it. Whoever chose these doors, chose well. They have polycarbonate glass which is almost completely impenetrable. Also, Mr. Norvell Jones came by a few minutes ago and gave me a radio so we can call for help immediately should the need arise. Once the students get here, I'll go over the new security measures they're instituting here so everyone will feel better, I think."

Soon, the students arrived on time and seemingly no worse for wear after yesterday's incident.

They had all settled into their classrooms when one of Ellie's GED men raised his hand with a question.

"Ms. Thomson, I'm Randolph and I have a question if you don't mind. You have all these degrees and experience in your job but you're dating a custodian. We have to wonder about that because it seems like even though he's a badass, excuse me, he's not on your level," Randolph finished, and the rest of his group nodded their heads in agreement."

"I guess I haven't had time to teach you about respect and the value of people yet, have I? A long time ago, I learned that you give people respect and they usually give it right back, even if you might not have known them well enough yet to earn it. Never judge people by how much money they make, their religion or their education.

Two of the smartest people I ever knew never went to school. What they lacked in book learning, they had in common sense. They were good judges of people and that doesn't come out of a book. People can get education and make more money, but religion is private and none of our business. We shouldn't miss out on friendships because people are different. Any job has value, and you should do your best whether you're the dishwasher at a fast food restaurant or the college president. Same thing. Give your best and you can be proud of the work you do. Alright, that's my philosophical lecture for today. Let's get to work!" Ellie said and saw that her group was thinking about her words and seemed to like what she'd said.

She hoped they listened and took it to heart because in order to be successful they were going to have to change old attitudes and habits or getting their GED wouldn't open the doors they were hoping for.

School settled into a routine with no further major incidents over the next week. The new teachers weren't naturals but did listen to Ellie's comments and tips. They watched her teach a few of her different lessons and tried to model their behavior after hers. Teaching was turning out to be much better than they'd thought when they started, even after that disastrous day that scared them all.

On Thursday before a long weekend, Noé came by to pick up Ellie as he always did

JJ Dayton   When the Basil Bolts

and had some news for her. "Graciela's
coming into town on her way to Austin this
Saturday. Can we have a gettogether at my
place? I'd like to meet your kids, and I'd
like Graciela to meet you, your kids and
Aunt Flo."

"That sounds like fun. I promised my
girls we would do just that one of these days
soon. Let's do that. Just tell me which day
and I'll get in touch with my crew."

"Ah, Ellie, isn't this weekend an
important date? I've been meaning to ask
you to be certain," Noé said significantly.

"Yes, this is the weekend when we find
out if I'm going to get my period or not.
Remember that I told you how unlikely even
worrying is? It's strange to be unmarried
and having this discussion with my
boyfriend whom I've been dating for less
than a month. It's so weird. You know it is.
Don't give me that look," Ellie said and
laughed.

"OK. I agree with part of what you said.
It is a little odd to be talking about your
periods with your boyfriend of less than a
month as you put it. However, we are where
we are in this process, both waiting for an
answer. Either way, I'm with you, Ellie.
Don't doubt that. Let's just accept what
happens and move forward. I care about

you; you know that even though we haven't said words of commitment, I am committed to you. *Venga lo que venga. Estoy contigo, mi amor.* (Come whatever comes, I'm with you, my love.)"

"Thank you, Noé. I think I needed to hear that just then. Text me as soon as you figure out with Graciela what time and which day. Auntie Flo and I have some baking to do either way."

"Ellie, you don't have to worry about the food. I'll have it catered. I'm sure I can find someone local even on very short notice to provide the food for us."

"But it wouldn't be a party if Flo and I didn't bake something to bring. Trust me on this. You don't want to miss our desserts," Ellie laughed as she explained why she would bake regardless of what Noé said about caterers.

Chapter 9: The Fiesta

It turned out that the party was Sunday and Graciela was flying in Saturday evening. Ellie baked her delicious brownies she brought to every party and Flo made both a peach and pecan pie. Ellie's kids met at her house, and they caravanned over to Noé's behind Ellie and Flo.

Noé met them outside in front of his house and they all came to stand in front of him. Ellie reached up to kiss his cheek and her kids came closer to be introduced. After the introductions, Graciela came through the door in her wheelchair, a closed look on her face.

"Ellie, I'd like you to meet my daughter Graciela and Graciela, this is Flo, Rachel,

Wendy, Trey and Mike, Ellie's aunt and her kids."

"Er, it's nice to meet you. There sure are a lot of you!"

"Gabby! Sé cortés. Esta es mi novia y su famila, (Be polite. This is my girlfriend and her family.)" Noé said with exasperation.

"I guess you're right about that Graciela. Maybe we are a little overwhelming. I promise that we're nice though if that helps deal with our numbers," Ellie said smilingly.

The awkward moment passed when Flo asked where to take their desserts. Noé led her to the dessert table on the patio. There was a large patio on the front to the side of the walk that was easy to navigate with a wheelchair. The stones and cement were recently laid, a project Noé had undertaken when he moved in to prepare the house for Graciela's accessibility. It looked like it would work fine as he watched his daughter wheel toward the drink table with Mike and Trey.

"Ellie, do you have a minute for me right now? They're still setting up the food. It'll be another ten minutes. I think our kids and your aunt can manage on their own for a few minutes. Yes?"

"Sure, let's go inside. I want to talk to you also."

They went to Noé's bedroom and sat down on the bed, looking at each other.

"OK. No more suspense. I didn't get my period yesterday and I'm crazy regular. Er, I brought a pregnancy test I'd like to take now in your bathroom if that's alright with you. Then we'll know. I bought one of those early detection kinds."

"Uh, sure, *mi amor*. I'm still processing the late period. Go ahead. I'll be here waiting." Noé encouraged.

Ellie went into the master bathroom and peed on the pregnancy test stick. It could take up to three minutes for her results, so she put the cap on and walked back into the room. Noé looked up at her expectantly and she held out the stick for him to see.

"It doesn't say anything, Ellie."

"Give it a minute, love. I just did it. She sat beside him on the bed, both their eyes glued to the window on the test stick. Just after Ellie sat down, a positive plus sign appeared in the window.

"We're pregnant!" Noé exclaimed as he engulfed Ellie in a tight hug. He turned her face to his and kissed her passionately till he noticed the taste of her tears.

"*Mi amor,* what's wrong? That's the best news. I'm happy. Very happy. Aren't you?"

"Yes, Noé I am. I just never thought this could happen to me. I've wanted this for years and now it's happening. These are happy tears. I'm happy too, Noé. You gave me something I've wanted my whole life, and I get to share this child with you. You're already a wonderful father and a wonderful man. Sharing a baby with you will be perfect."

"Ah, *mi amor*. I can't tell you how happy I am that we will share this child together. You already are the best parent and I'm glad that I could give you your dream."

Fin/End